Webb's Wondrous Tales
Book 1

Webb's Wondrous Tales
Book 1

Mack H. Webb, Jr.
Illustrations by Celia Webb

Pilinut Press, Inc.

Webb's Wondrous Tales
Book 1
First Edition

Book and cover design by Celia Webb

Pilinut Press, Inc.
www.pilinutpress.com

The Pilinut is the edible seed of the *Canarium ovatum* tree which is native to Southeast Asia. Tasting like sweet almonds, it is eaten for its health benefits including prevention of anemia and for nourishment of the brain and nervous system.

Library of Congress Control Number: 2006932530
Printed in Warrenton, Virginia

ISBN 0-9779576-1-6

TABLE OF CONTENTS:

Dedication

To my parents, Mack H. Webb, Sr. and Ruth Mae Webb, who fueled my imagination.

Anita the Artist

*A*nita loves works of art. So much so that she decides to pursue life as an artist. Anita apprentices with masters in the arts of sculpting and painting. It is a lot of hard work, but in time she becomes a very accomplished artist.

Anita goes forth with her newly acquired skills, to make her fortune. Her plan is to open her own studio when she earns enough money. In the meantime, she makes a living by traveling and doing portraits.

It is while she is traveling, that she meets a man in a hooded cloak. He is sitting on a patch of grass at the edge of a pond, and sobbing softly.

Anita's first instinct is to paint the figure and call it, "Hooded Weeper On Sward". But no! This scene touches Anita's heart. She inquires of the man, "Pray, why are you filled with such sadness."

The man sniffs a couple of times before launching into a tale of woe that details the cause of his plaintive and melancholy mood. "I must wear this hood," laments the man, "because I look hideous. It is a curse inflicted by an evil wizard. On my honor, I did nothing to incur his wrath. It is just my bad

1

luck. The wizard has warned me that should I ever gaze at my reflection, I will be instantly turned into stone."

"Is there no cure for this spell?" asks Anita.

"Well…" answers the man, "The wizard promises to lift the spell if I pay him. However, I have given him a great sum already without receiving satisfaction. What can I do?" The man beats his chest in frustration and futility. "Why should this unlucky thing happen to me," he moans, "after I have been so careful? I never walk under ladders, I never let a black cat cross my path, and I always toss a little salt over my shoulder for luck."

"Please," says Anita in a soothing voice, "do not be so hard on yourself. I would like to help you if I can. My name is Anita, what may I call you?"

The man lifts his head a bit and replies, "My name is Chardonnay."

Anita suspects the wizard is actually a swindler, out to make some easy money. She also suspects that Chardonnay's superstitious nature has made him an easy target. Anita asks Chardonnay to allow her to see his face.

After much hesitation, Chardonnay complies. "Alright," says Chardonnay, "but remember, you asked for it." He takes a deep breath and tosses back his hood.

Anita gasps involuntarily.

"See!" says Chardonnay quickly replacing his hood, "I warned you."

"No!" says Anita. "It isn't what you think. Here, wait a moment." Anita takes out a drawing pad and quickly sketches a likeness of what she has seen. When she is finished, she turns the pad so that Chardonnay might see a drawing of his face.

Chardonnay is reluctant to look, but curiosity wins him over. His eyes dart to the sketchpad, and he inhales sharply. "This cannot be," he says in a hoarse whisper. "It is my face...my face before the curse."

"It is your face after the curse," says Anita, "for the wizard is nothing more than a swindler. He uses your superstitious nature to fill his purse with your coin."

Chardonnay is stunned to find that he has been so deceived. Still, he fears that the swindler will pursue him if he does not give him the money he demands.

"As you can see, I am not very robust," says Chardonnay. "However, the swindler is a mountain of a man. I am not ashamed to admit that I would not be his equal in combat. I see no other way but to pay him."

"Do not worry," says Anita, "I have a plan that will free you from him once and for all."

Anita visits a local merchant to purchase the things she will need to carry out her plan. It takes her two full days to make everything ready.

"Today is the day that the wizard, uh swindler, is to meet me at the pond for his payment," says Chardonnay. "He will be angry if I am not there."

"There is no need to fret about him," says Anita. "He won't be bothering you again. I've made sure of that."

Chardonnay is grateful that Anita happened by, and that she has taken it upon herself to help him.

"Now that you are free to travel where you please," Anita continues, "where will you go?"

"Italy," says Chardonnay. "I come from a very wealthy family, the Vino family. We own the largest vineyards and wineries in all of Italy. I was ashamed to go home when I thought I was doomed to hide my face forever, beneath the folds of a hood. Now that you have been so kind as to help me, I can and shall return to my beloved Italy. I would be most honored, Anita, if you would accompany me. I will introduce you to the great artists Italy has to offer."

"I would like that," replies Anita. "Italy is renowned for its artists, and I am sure I will learn a lot from them."

Anita and Chardonnay stroll away arm-in-arm.

Meanwhile the swindler, looking to collect another purse of coins from Chardonnay, arrives at the pond. He grins wickedly when he sees the familiar hooded cloak. "I like it that you are so prompt," he says to the cloaked figure. "It's that time again. Time to pay up!"

The swindler receives no reply.

"Hey!" growls the swindler, "I'm talking to you, whelp." He strides over, yanks the hood from the figure's head, yelps in astonishment, stumbles back and falls onto his haunches. The open-mouthed swindler is horrified by what he sees, for before him, gazing into a looking glass, is a solid stone Chardonnay. ≡

Beanstalk
(Inspired by the traditional folktale "Jack and the Beanstalk")

Many years ago, a tiny boy visited Giant Land. He did so by way of a beanstalk grown from magic beans.

Having climbed the beanstalk, the boy then absconded with many of Giant Land's precious artifacts. Included in the theft were a magic harp and a goose that laid golden eggs.

To be sure, the items stolen were irreplaceable and it saddened the folk of Giant Land. However, what really cast a dark cloud over Giant Land was the loss of the king's son, the prince.

The prince, who had the ability to smell trouble, had ferreted out the tiny boy and pursued him in an effort to save Giant Land's national treasures. Such was the prince's determination to win the day that he trailed the youth down the beanstalk.

Once on the ground, the wicked waif grabbed a razor-sharp axe and commenced to hew through the thick base of the beanstalk.

The prince was a little more then halfway down the beanstalk, when he felt it shudder violently. Bewildered and a little frightened, the prince clung to the vine. The shuddering continued rhythmically until the beanstalk began to list. The prince could do nothing as the ground rushed to meet him.

That fateful day was the last anyone in Giant Land saw of the prince.

Needless to say, the king and queen were devastated at the loss of their son. The king, determined never to be caught off guard again, deployed sentries to patrol constantly for encroaching beanstalks.

The sentries marched all over Giant Land, alert and ever watchful, for a while at least. When for a long time nothing else happened, they became lax. Even now we find the evening guard sleeping. This is most unfortunate, for it is this night that a beanstalk makes its appearance.

The beanstalk's questing tendrils poke through the clouds, and moments later, so do a band of tiny men. The grouping is led by none other than the boy, now a man, who had years before stolen the magic harp and goose. Tonight's beanstalk is the result of the last magic bean he possessed. As it is with all ill-gotten gains, they never last long. Having frittered away his plunder, he is back for more.

With sacks slung over their shoulders, the hooligans make their way toward the castle. They creep by the dozing sentry, and then they move more swiftly, fueled by the thought of becoming wealthy men. And this time there will be no interference from the prince who, by the way, is still alive...

The prince, though bruised and battered, had survived his plunge to the earth. He had lain in pain for some time, until a kindly physician encountered him. The physician secluded the giant prince and nursed him back to health. Nursing the prince back to health was the easy part. Keeping the prince fed and watered was more difficult. Great amounts of food and drink had to be gathered daily. By the end of each day the physician's legs were shaky and his back was very sore.

The prince relayed to the physician the details of his fall to earth, and inquired how he might return to his home in the clouds.

The physician could only shake his head and shrug his shoulders. He had heard of the towering beanstalk, but had no idea how to grow such a plant.

The prince was disappointed, but he resolved to bide his time and not give up hope. His patience is rewarded.

Late one evening, the physician trots to the hiding place of the prince. In the years that the physician has served the prince, the prince seems not to have aged at all. The same cannot be said of the physician, for he has aged greatly, and is quite short of breath when he arrives. "St-...St-...Stalk! Bean...Beanstalk!" the old physician manages to say between wheezing gasps. Mustering his energies he bellows, "Giant beanstalk, over there! Hurry!", while pointing in the direction from which he had come.

The prince does hurry, but not before thanking the physician. "Your kindness, devotion, and generosity shall not be forgotten," promises the prince. "In two days time come again to this spot."

"Yes-yes," says the old physician, rather embarrassed and impatiently. "Get thee gone whilst thy route home still stands!"

Bounding strides have the prince at the base of the beanstalk in a moment's time. Grasping the stalk, he begins to climb.

Meanwhile, within the king's castle, tiny crooks are stuffing their sacks with loot. Soon the sacks are so stuffed that their seams threaten to rip. The thieves hoist the sacks and make for the beanstalk. They slip past everyone, including the still napping sentry.

As they near the beanstalk they chuckle low in their throats. They are amused at how easy it has been to pillage the foolish giants. So imagine their surprise, when the prince pokes his head above the clouds.

"Ah-ha! Little wretches!" roars the prince. "This time I have you!"

The prince scoops up the tiny men and strides to the castle. The king and queen embrace their son joyously, and then they mete out justice on the tiny men. Their fate is swiftly decided, and the king summons the court magician.

The magician turns the tiny scoundrels into a gaggle of fat geese. As you can imagine, the rascals feel quite miserable about the outcome of their venture, for they had thought to test their luck by raiding the giant's castle, but their luck has failed them. Now they are sent out into the world where it is doubtful they will be any luckier at eluding hunters and foxes.

Justice has been served, but the prince has another matter to attend to. The prince gives the order that a massive quantity of string be brought to him. The string is brought in a sufficient length for the prince's needs. Using a clever knot, he ties one end of the string to the handle of a small basket. He lowers the basket to the spot where he had bid the physician return. When the basket reaches the earth, the prince gives the string a sharp tug. The tug releases the string from the basket, and the prince hauls up the string.

Shortly thereafter, the old physician arrives at the basket. Within the basket is a large vial, on which is written, "Drink Me!" The old physician swigs the vial's contents and instantly becomes young and vivacious. Further exploration of the basket yields a heap of gold and precious jewels of every type.

There is also a letter for the young physician from the prince, it reads: "Good Friend Physician, I shall always be in your debt. Live long and prosper." And so he does. ≡

Brock and Sam Throw Down Their Hats

One warm, sunny day, Brock and Sam set out on the road with a cartload of apples. They hope to sell their harvest in the town market for a tidy sum.

On the road they pass many sorcerers. The sorcerers are on their way to the Annual Sorcerer's Convention held in a nearby cove. Brock and Sam step carefully so as not to unwittingly anger the mystic travelers.

Presently, they spy a copper coin lying near the side of the road. They both rush over to pick it up.

"Look at what I have found!" exclaims Brock.

"What you have found?" returns Sam. "I saw it first!"

"No you didn't!" retorts Brock, taking off his hat and throwing it to the ground.

"Ohhhh, yes I did!" snarls Sam, taking off his hat and throwing it likewise to the ground.

As they stand arguing, the horse continues to draw the cart down the road.

Brock and Sam, when they finally pause for breath, notice that the horse and cart are nowhere in sight. Immediately, they run down the road until they become exhausted from their efforts. It is of no use. Horse, cart, and apples have all vanished and, along with them, the money Brock and Sam had hoped to receive.

Brock and Sam feel quite foolish for having so carelessly lost the fruits of their labors. They retrieve their hats, and look at each other rather sheepishly as they dust them off. Brock extends his hand and displays the copper coin. "Here," says Brock to Sam. "I think you did see it first."

"No," says Sam, "I am certain that it was your gaze that fell upon it before mine."

They clasp each other's hand and vow never to argue again, but to be as brothers henceforth.

Since they have no apples to sell, Brock and Sam decide that fishing might land them something they could sell at market. So they load up their fishing boat with tackle, nets, and other provisions. They prepare to shove off.

"Okay, Brock," says Sam, "it's your turn to row. Grab the oars and bend your back."

"My turn?" questions Brock.

"Yes," says Sam. "The last time we went out, it was my back and arms that got sore from rowing."

"That was me doing the rowing," says Brock, "and my arms still ache from the effort!"

"This is no time to be a slug," roars Sam, throwing his hat to the ground. "You will row and that's final!"

"I will not," bellows Brock, snatching off his hat and throwing it to the ground.

While they are thus engaged, the boat along with their tackle, nets, and provisions drifts out to sea. By the time they notice what has happened, their boat is but a speck on the horizon.

Queasiness envelops them as they gaze wide-eyed and open-mouthed after their boat.

They retrieve the hats and brush them off, all the while feeling like a couple of nincompoops.

They look at each other sheepishly. "Maybe you are right," owns Brock, "it was my turn to row the boat."

"No," says Sam, "on further reflection, I am sure it was my turn."

They clap each other on the shoulder and vow never to argue again, but to be as brothers henceforth.

Brotherly love is short lived for Brock and Sam, and it isn't long before they are again hotly contesting another topic. Their hats are in the dust at their feet, and they bark and screech with much heat and fervor. They go on at great length, ignoring the fact that their throats have become sore and their voices are mere croaks.

Their quarrel rouses a sorcerer, who has propped himself against a boulder in an effort to catch a few winks. He is in an ill temper, for during the Annual Sorcerer's Convention, he placed very badly in the Sorcerer's Cup finals. He may have had problems landing the Sorcerer's Cup, but he has no problems turning Brock and Sam into a couple of toads.

So immersed are Brock and Sam in their dispute, that they take no notice of their change in form. And if you listen on warm summer nights, you can still hear them loudly croaking their arguments. ≡

Brock and Sam Throw Down Their Hats

Can You Keep A Secret?

*T*his is little Ricky. Ricky was born with very large ears. They grew and grew. Now, Ricky has the ability to hear the faintest conversations from miles away.

Ricky was once looked upon as a charmingly sweet little boy. That all changed when little Ricky learned to talk.

Ricky overhears everything. Ricky tells everything he overhears. He cannot keep a secret no matter how hard he tries. Truth be told, Ricky never tries very hard. He feels it is his solemn duty to keep everyone well informed.

Ricky lives in the town of Getcrackin. It used to be a bustling town full of life, activity, and conversations. Now it resembles a ghost town. The streets are empty, and people go out only when it is absolutely necessary. They stay indoors with their shutters firmly closed, in the hopes that little Ricky will not overhear their muffled conversations.

Finally, the townspeople can take their isolation no longer. They approach the mayor with the demand that he do something about little Ricky.

The mayor says he will try to think of something. Weeks pass and the mayor is still at a loss as to what can be done. In truth, the mayor considers running little Ricky out of town. But no, that is too cruel a thought. Ricky is not a bad boy, he just…talks too much of what he overhears.

The town seems destined to spend a long time in lockdown and silence. Until one day a traveling wizard comes to town. He wonders why the streets are so devoid of people. He knows there are people in this town. He can see eyes peering at him from cracked shutters.

The wizard continues until he reaches the center of town. There he begins to perform all manner of tricks and conjuring. Ever so slowly, the townsfolk begin to emerge. They cluster around the wizard, gazing in wonder at his arts.

At length the wizard finishes his display to a hearty round of applause and cheers.

He inquires why the townspeople bar themselves inside their houses.

The townspeople tell the wizard of little Ricky and the predicament his large ears put them in.

The wizard thinks for a moment, while stroking his long beard. Then he says he may have a solution to their problem.

The townspeople can hardly believe their good fortune.

The wizard says that first he must see the local confection-maker. The wizard instructs the confectioner to mix up a batch of candy according to his instructions. When the candy is done, the wizard waves his wand over the candy and, KAZOW, all is complete.

The next day, little Ricky is strolling down the street when he meets the confection-maker. Smiling, the confection-maker presents Ricky with a sack of his latest sweet creation.

Ricky is overjoyed. He opens his mouth to say something, but the moment he utters the first sound, a piece of candy leaps from the sack and into Ricky's mouth. Ricky begins to chew, and chew, and chew. The candy is a taffy so chewy and sticky, that little Ricky is unable to say anything. He can only mumble and chew.

The confectioner asks Ricky if there is something he wants to say.

Ricky certainly does! But every time he tries to speak, another piece of candy hurls itself into Ricky's mouth. Ricky tries to hand the sack back, but it seems to be stuck to his fingers. Henceforth, it is to be Ricky's constant companion.

The townspeople are pleased that they can return to their former hustle and bustle.

They are also pleased with the sweet way in which Ricky keeps a secret. ≡

Comet the Cat

On Farmer Griby's farm, there lives a cat named Comet. Comet has acquired the reputation of being an unsurpassed ratter. He keeps the rats out of the farmer's grain, stored garden produce, and outbuildings. Comet enjoys this activity, and does it without thought of reward.

One day, while he is pursuing a rat through a horse barn, a startled horse kicks Comet. The blow knocks the wind out of the cat. As Comet lay prostrate, the rat escapes.

"Useless cat!" whinnies the horse, unapologetically. "Stay out of my stall! Do your rat chasing elsewhere."

Comet, still feeling weak from the kick he has received, drags himself away to lick his wounds.

In time, Comet makes a full recovery and is once again earning his keep by ridding the farm of rats. A rat creeps into the hen house, in the hopes of having a meal of eggs or sleeping chickens. Comet, ever vigilant, sees the intruder and gives chase.

The noise of the chase startles the sleeping chickens into wakefulness. Upon seeing Comet in their coop, the chickens think he is up to mischief and so attack him.

Comet, pecked and scratched to within an inch of his life, hurries from the hen house. He limps to a spot beneath the farmhouse porch, and licks his wounds.

While recuperating under the porch, a scratching sound causes Comet to prick-up his ears. Upon investigation, Comet finds a rat making its way into the farmhouse kitchen. A chase ensues within the kitchen. The commotion brings the farmer's wife who, taking up a broom, beats Comet from the kitchen. The rat, unnoticed by the farmer's wife, escapes unscathed.

The beating Comet received from the farmer's wife caused him little pain, but it did hurt his feline feelings. Comet, only trying to do his job, is mistreated and scorned at every turn. So Comet resolves to give up chasing rats, as no one appreciates the efforts he makes on their behalf.

Once Comet retires, the rats become bold and numerous. The rats swagger through the farmyard as though they own the place. They gorge themselves on grain and pilfer from the pantry. They enjoy eggs from the hen house, and hangout in the horse barn where they agitate the horses by nipping at their heels. Comet watches all of this with disinterest.

A day arrives when the horse pays a visit to Comet. "Mr. Cat," neighs the horse, "I apologize for kicking you. You may chase rats through the horse barn anytime you please."

"We, too, are sorry for attacking you in the hen house," clucks a flock of chickens. "We should have known you were just doing your job."

"I was wrong to beat you from the kitchen with my broom," says the farmer's wife, as she places a saucer of sweet milk before Comet. "Please go back to what you do so well, and get rid of these rats."

Comet looks at all of his visitors in turn, and then laps up the milk. Just as he finishes the milk, a plump rat saunters over to him.

The rat has become swollen with boldness as well as cheese. "Stupid cat!" sneers the rat. "I have a mind to..."

The fat rat's words are cut short, as Comet pounces and makes short work of it. This act does not escape the notice of the other rats. They scatter pell-mell with Comet in hot pursuit.

It is a day that will be talked about around the farm, and remembered for years to come. However, it will not be the rats that recount the tale. For when the sun sets on Griby's farm, not a single rat remains.

Comet is indeed an unsurpassed ratter! ≡

The Corn Patch

Master Kennick is a wealthy and very unpleasant landowner. Today he has ordered some of his servants to drive his wagon into town. The wagon is filled with ears of dried corn. The corn is to be sold at the town market. Master Kennick hopes it will make him a lot of money.

As Master Kennick's servants bump along in the wagon, they tear into an enormous basket of victuals. They stuff themselves with sandwiches, cheese, cake, savory pies, fruit, and ale.

They are still eating ravenously, when they meet a poor man standing by the roadside. He asks of them a few crumbs of bread.

The servants guffaw maliciously for they are wicked of heart, just like the master they serve. They pummel the poor fellow with ears of dried corn. Then, howling with laughter, they continue their journey into town.

The poor man looks at the mound of corn that lies at his feet. He is delighted by how generous the servants have been. Gathering up the ears, he heads home.

27

Some of the corn is ground into cornmeal. Using the husks, he fashions sandals that he will sell for a few coppers a pair. The rest of the corn kernels he saves for planting.

Upon their return, the wicked servants regale Master Kennick with the story of the poor man, and his plea for crumbs.

Master Kennick is outraged. How dare someone hinder his load of corn, and so delay money for his coffers.

Master Kennick, being a mean-spirited individual, enjoys heaping mischief on others. So he demands that cartloads of manure, from his horse stables, be dumped on the poor man's doorstep. Master Kennick, wants to show the poor wretch just where he sits in the scheme of things.

In the morning, the poor man can smell a strong aroma of something outside his front door. He opens the door on the largest heap of horse manure he has ever seen. There it steams, right on his doorstep.

He is thrilled. He cannot believe his good fortune. What, he wonders, has he done to deserve such a gift? For manure, in such a quantity, is just what he needs to prepare his garden for planting.

He wishes he knew the name of his benefactor, he would surely thank him for this bounty.

Hiding behind a tree, unseen by the poor man, is one of Kennick's servants. This servant relays the poor man's reaction to his master.

On hearing how gleeful the poor man is, Master Kennick becomes furious.

Master Kennick orders the poor man's field be set aflame.

Returning from a trip into town, the poor man sees that all of the vegetation has been burned from his field.

The poor man is shocked. He wonders who would do such a thing? What thoughtful person would spare him the back-breaking labor of hoeing the weeds from this field. The poor man is very happy. Now he can plant his corn seeds.

Master Kennick is livid when he hears of the poor man's happiness. He must, he reflects, devise a more fiendish deed to place upon the poor man's head.

At night, Master Kennick's servants sneak into the poor man's shed. They find a sack of corn kernels. Thinking its intended purpose is for making corn meal, they take the sack and fling its contents far and wide across the poor man's field. This done, they scurry back to their master.

The morning comes, and the poor man is ready to plant his corn. Look where he might, he can not locate the sack of corn. With a heavy spirit he walks over to his field. His spirits are immediately lifted when he sees that his corn has already been spread over his field. Oh, wonder of wonders!

That he should be visited by such good fortune is hard to believe. Whistling a lively tune, he lightly covers the seeds with soil.

The corn is up and growing well, when the crop is beset by a host of insects. The poor man is at a loss for what to do.

Meanwhile, Master Kennick is out surveying his holding when he sees some servants trying to shoo geese from a garden patch. It seems that the geese are eating every green thing in sight. This gives Master Kennick an idea.

He orders fifty geese to be taken to the poor man's cornfield. Surely the geese will eat the corn plants all the way down to the roots. He chuckles to himself as he imagines the poor man's impending sorrow.

The geese scramble about the corn field. However, instead of eating the corn plants, they gorge themselves on the hoards of insects plaguing the poor man's crop. The geese eat until every last insect is consumed. When they are done, they are so stuffed they can hardly move.

Master Kennick's plan of mischief fails yet again. This puts him in a grim mood.

Weeks pass, and the poor man's corn has grown up straight and strong.

During the night, while the poor man sleeps, Master Kennick sends his servants to cut down every cornstalk in the poor man's field. It is Master Kennick's last chance to ruin the poor man's crop of corn.

In the morning, the poor man goes to his field. Today he will harvest his corn crop. Upon seeing his cornfield, he stops dead in his tracks. Surely his eyes deceive him. Every cornstalk lays on the ground, for they have been cut at the roots.

The poor man's eyes fill with tears. If he only knew who has done this thing, he would thank him heartily! At every turn this corn patch has met with good fortune. Now, someone has been kind enough to save him the trouble of cutting a field of cornstalks.

He gathers the stalks, takes them to his house, and stacks the corn in a cart. Some he keeps to eat, some he will keep as seeds for next year's crop, the rest he will sell at the town market.

At the market, he sells his corn for a very good price.

The poor man is no longer poor. He is wealthy, and known throughout the land for his kindness.

What of Master Kennick? He is enraged that his scheming has helped the poor man become wealthier than even he is. In a fit of anger, Master Kennick fires all of his servants. With no servants to tend his holdings, they quickly fall into an unprofitable state. Eventually, the master leaves his lands a very poor man. He is never heard from again. ≡

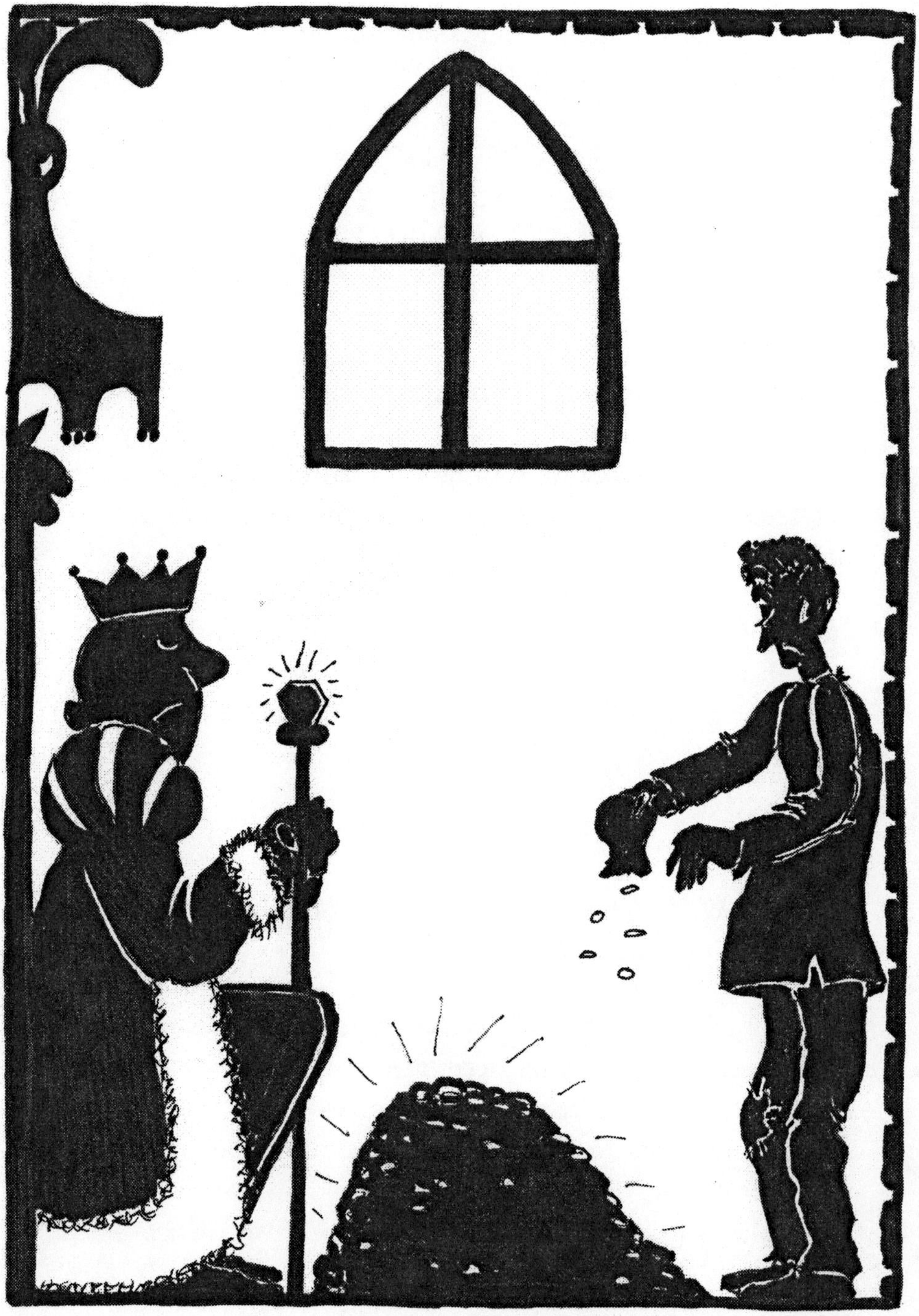

Doors to Fortune

King Hoard is always thinking of new ways to tax his subjects. Of course, there are the usual taxes such as the land tax and the property tax, but the king has some unusual taxes as well. There is the "walking upright" tax, the sleeping tax, the tooth tax, the "breathing air" tax, and for those who try to avoid breathing, there is the death tax.

As you can imagine, King Hoard is not without his troubles. The king frets over how to protect his wealth from others. He tosses and turns in his bed at night, as nightmares visit him. The nightmares are of thieves stealing away with his riches.

King Hoard decides to have a new treasure room built for his wealth. The room is to be constructed of the stoutest stone, and the king himself will design the doors. Construction begins at once.

The stonemasons, being rather slow in their construction processes, are not very far along when the treasure-room doors arrive.

The doors are massive, ornate works wrought by master craftsmen. The unfinished treasure room is a good place to store them until they can be hung. When the door-makers attempt to do this, the stonemasons become angry.

"Don't bring those doors in here!" shouts the head stonemason. "How are we to do our work properly, when you clutter our space with your doors? Store them someplace else."

The door-makers have no choice; reluctantly they place the doors outside where they will be out of the stonemason's way.

Towards evening, the king arrives at the treasure room's construction site. He sees the treasure-room doors against the hillocks. It displeases him greatly that his custom-crafted doors are being treated in such a manner. He has the head stonemason placed under arrest, but changes his mind when the mason explains.

"Sire," pleads the head stonemason as he mops his brow with a tattered piece of cloth, "I fear that falling stone may accidentally damage the doors if they are left inside."

"A wise decision," reflects the king. "I had these doors especially made for my new treasure room. If they are to be outside, I will not take the chance that they might be molested or stolen. Therefore, I want them guarded around the clock. I forbid anyone to touch them without my permission." Having made his decree, the king departs.

Shortly after the king's departure, the captain of the guard arrives with two soldiers for each door. The soldiers will stand guard until they are replaced in twelve hours.

"Guard these doors well," warns the captain of the guard, "for they lead to the king's treasure rooms."

As it happens, a skirmish arises between King Hoard and a neighboring king. King Hoard imposes two more taxes, the eating tax and the "going to the restroom" tax, to cover the cost of his campaign.

For the time being, construction of the new treasure room is abandoned.

In time, the king successfully defends his realm against the invaders. The experience leaves King Hoard seriously ill. The king receives a further blow, when he learns the coffers are empty.

This is troublesome news. The king knows that he will not last much longer, and so sends for his eldest son, Prince Upright.

The prince arrives, and he is shaken by his father's depleted state of health. He leans close to his father's lips, that he might hear his whispered words.

"The doors," rasps the king weakly, "the doors to the treasure rooms...they will save the kingdom. For...in them…you will f-find g-go—." Before the king can finish his words, he expires.

When Prince Upright finally exits his father's chambers, he finds the hallway packed with anxious onlookers.

"My father the king," announces the prince, "is no more. But he has given me the knowledge and the means to save the kingdom. He told me that now is the time to open the doors to the treasure rooms. Therefore, gather oxen and carts, so that we may transport the wealth we find therein."

A parade of townsfolk follows the procession of oxcarts to the treasure room doors. When they arrive at their destination, the doors are pried up.

There is a collective intake of breath, for there is nothing behind the doors except bare earth. They try digging to unearth an entrance, but the only thing they unearth is more earth.

"That's it then," pronounces Prince Upright, "the kingdom is ruined."

"Hey," says someone in the milling crowd, "those doors ought to be worth something!"

The Prince walks over to examine a door. The prying tools have scratched away some of the brown paint, and at that scratch the door shines golden. More paint is removed and it is found that the doors consist of solid gold and silver.

The onlookers cheer wildly. The realm is saved.

Prince Upright has the doors smelted and struck into coin. The coins are distributed to the impoverished townsfolk.

When Prince Upright is crowned king, he does away with the "walking upright" tax, the sleeping tax, the tooth tax, the "breathing air" tax, and the death tax. He also abolishes the eating tax and the "going to the restroom" tax. The people of the realm live happily and prosper, and so does King Upright. ≡

Drago the Dreaded Dragon

This is Drago Mountain. It is named after Drago, the dreaded dragon that dwells within it.

Why is Drago so dreaded? Is it because his every step sets the whole countryside quaking? Is it because his hide is comprised of 12-inch thick, iron-tuff scales? Maybe it is because his teeth are needle sharp and longer than your arm. Could it be Drago's roar, which can defoliate trees? Is he dreaded because he sometimes takes to the sky on giant, leathery wings? In truth, it might be his breath, for it is fire and brimstone.

Drago inhabited this region long before humans settled in the valley below. At first, it was just a few people living in the valley. Drago did not mind, and so kept his presence unknown. However, more and more people began to populate the valley. They built great houses and other structures that required massive amounts of wood. They began to strip the countryside of its trees. Soon, the people threatened to invade his sanctuary as well. It was then that Drago decided to make an appearance.

Now, Drago is feared throughout the land. So afraid are the townspeople, that the king has offered half of his kingdom to the knight that eliminates Drago. Many knights have tried to win the prize, but all have met with the same fate.

Drago has a mountain of armor outside the entrance to his cave. It is the armor once worn by the finest knights the realm had to offer. Charred bones lie strewn outside his dwelling. Is it any wonder people fear Drago? It is just as Drago would have it, for it keeps people away from his domain. He is always alone. He is happy. Or is he?

Poor Drago. He hates that he has to carry on a charade for his safety's sake. He is not really the terrible dragon everyone thinks he is. If anyone could get close enough to know the dragon within, he would find a gentle, intelligent, and caring beast.

Uh-oh, here comes another knight who would try to obtain half of the King's kingdom. The knight is riding proud and upright, on his noble steed. How shiny and pristine his armor is. Will he fare better than the rest?

The knight must cross a fetid swamp if he would do battle with the dragon. After a moment's hesitation, he enters the putrid slime pit. Emerging on the other side, he finds himself covered in filth. The stench of stinky, sticky mud and goo is overwhelming. The knight reels, and is forced to doff his armor and wash himself in a nearby sulfurous lake.

While the knight bathes, Drago quietly creeps in and makes off with the knight's armor and weaponry. Then he roars with all of his might, blows smoke, and stomps around shaking trees.

The knight, upon hearing the roar, turns bleach white. Giving no thought to his armor or weapons, he takes flight with all of the speed his horse can muster.

Drago adds the knight's armor to his already large heap.

Winter arrives in the valley in the form of a terrible blizzard. The snow and sleet fall fast and heavy. The valley is quickly buried under snow and ice. Then the temperature plummets to well below freezing. Unable to get out of their houses for food or supplies, it looks as though the inhabitants are doomed.

Meanwhile, Drago is heating stones until they are red hot; then he tosses them into the sulfur lake until it roils. He then slips into the water to soak and think.

Drago is not bothered by the blizzard. He has weathered winters much worse than this. However, Drago imagines the people in the valley must be in a bad way.

When the blizzard abates, Drago makes his way to the valley. He finds that only roofs show above the snow and ice.   He knows that he must do something if the townspeople are to survive. Because he has a kind heart towards all living things, he acts at once.

Taking a deep breath, Drago exhales fire and brimstone over the valley. He is careful to keep the flames high enough to prevent incinerating the town. It is but a moment's work to defrost the valley and release the townspeople from their glacial prison.

The town is quick to show Drago their gratitude. The king lifts the bounty on Drago's head and erects a monument in his honor. The king also decrees that Drago's sanctuary will be guarded by the realm, and maintained in its natural state, as Drago would have it.

Drago is celebrated as the fiery dragon that saved a town from extinction. But even more celebrated is the therapeutic water found at Drago's hot springs resort. ≡

Drago the Dreaded Dragon

The Enchanted Cauldron

Thomas and his wife are destitute and sorely in need of money. The only thing they have to sell is a large black cauldron. Over the years they have used this pot to cook haunches of meat, savory stews, and lately, gruel. The meals they prepare now are so meager a small saucepan will suffice. Therefore, it is decided that Thomas will take the cauldron into town and sell it in the marketplace. If he haggles shrewdly, maybe he will get a few copper coins in exchange for it.

Thomas gets an early start the next morning, for it is a long way to the marketplace. His wife gives him a bundle containing an extravagant meal of stale bread and hard, moldy cheese. After thanking his wife, Thomas carefully places the bundle inside the cauldron. He straps the cauldron onto his back and begins his journey.

Several hours pass before Thomas feels the effects of not having eaten today. His stomach growls and cramps in protest of his self-induced famine. His knees buckle uncooperatively. Thomas decides he dare not wait any longer to eat. He gets the bundle from inside the cauldron, and consumes the bread and cheese with great relish. It is a veritable banquet, for half-starved Thomas.

Thomas soon regains some strength. Taking up the cauldron, he continues to march. It is not long before Thomas comes to a stretch of forest. He has no great desire to enter this forest, for he knows that it is home to wild and terrible beasts. It is also the shortest way to the town. Cautiously he creeps into the forest, whipping his head left or right at the slightest sound. As the foliage of the trees blots out the sun's light, Thomas quickens his pace. It is by sheer coincidence that the bear and Thomas see each other at the same moment.

The bear charges. It moves with incredible speed for one so massive.

Thomas moves a shade faster. He strips the cauldron from his back, leaps into it, and secures the lid.

The bear bats and rolls the cauldron around for a very long time before losing interest and shambling off.

The cauldron has been armor against the bear's attack. When Thomas crawls out of the cauldron, he is shaken but unharmed. Not wanting to risk another encounter with the bear, he races through the forest as fast as his legs will carry him.

Soon the forest is some distance behind Thomas. He flops onto the ground at the side of the road, for he must rest a while. Thomas is still catching his breath, when a wealthy nobleman in a carriage happens by.

The nobleman is feeling magnanimous. He flips a golden coin into Thomas' cauldron.

Thomas is so overwhelmed by his good fortune that he almost faints. He retrieves the golden coin, that he might examine it. Never before has he beheld so beautiful an object. He secrets the coin on his person and continues on his way. It is growing dark, and he desires to be in the town by nightfall.

Well after the sun has set, Thomas is still making his way along the road. It is most unfortunate, for a brigand waylays him.

"Ah, what have we here?" coos the brigand. "Is it a goose ripe for the plucking? Give me all that you have of value and I might let you go unharmed."

"All that I have of value is this enchanted cauldron," says Thomas.

"Enchanted cauldron?" laughs the brigand. "What pray is it that makes this ordinary cook pot enchanted?"

"I'll tell you," answers Thomas. "This cauldron transforms into a suit of impenetrable armor. The cauldron provides me with a banquet when I am suffering from famine. And a golden coin appears in it as if by magic."

The brigand is enraptured by what he hears. At the mention of gold, his mouth goes dry, his breathing becomes ragged, and his palms perspire. "I will have this enchanted cauldron," announces the brigand. "Hand it over. Hand it over quickly or you shall regret it."

"If you harm me or try to take the cauldron by force," warns Thomas, "it will lose its enchantment. The cauldron must be willingly given. I shall not easily part with a prize such as this."

The brigand threatens and rants until his face is red and sweaty. It affords him nothing, for Thomas will not be swayed.

"A pox on you!" spits the brigand as he digs deeply into his purse. He counts out six golden coins. "Is this inducement enough for you to part with your wretched cauldron?" inquires the brigand.

"Well," says Thomas, "it means an awful lot to me…"

"Now who is the thief?" bellows the brigand angrily as he counts out another three golden coins.

"You drive a hard bargain," bemoans Thomas, "but it is a deal. The enchanted cauldron is yours."

The brigand snatches up the cauldron. Believing that he has come out ahead in the bargain, he rides swiftly into the night.

Thomas is heavier by ten golden coins upon reaching the town. He will eat well tonight. It seems that the cauldron was enchanted after all. ≡

The Fisherman's Wish

(Inspired by "The Fisherman and His Wife" by the Brothers Grimm)

T here once was a fisherman, who caught a truly magnificent fish.

The fish, realizing the seriousness of its plight, spoke to the fisherman. "If you would be so kind as to release me," said the fish, "I will repay your kindness, by granting your heart's desire." The fish could do it too, for it had extraordinary powers.

"Oh," said the fisherman, "there is no need to repay me. I'm happy to let you go. I could not bring myself to eat such a fine and noble-looking fish as yourself."

He returned the fish to its watery home. The fisherman took up his oars, and rowed his boat back to shore. When he arrived home empty-handed, his wife flew into a rage. He tried to calm her by telling of the encounter with the fish. This only made matters worse.

"Why didn't you ask for a fine house," she railed. "Go back to the fish and tell him to give us a fine place to live."

So the fisherman rowed his boat to the spot where he had released the fish.

The fish asked the fisherman why he looked so sad.

"It's my wife," replied the fisherman, "my wife sent me to ask you for a fine place to live."

"Go back to your wife," said the fish. "Her desire has been granted."

The fisherman returned home to find his former house gone, and in its place, an expanse of salty sea.

His wife was quite angry with him. She ordered him to go back, and tell the fish that she wanted a big house made of wood, not water!

Finding the fish at the same spot as before, the fisherman told the fish of his wife's demand.

"I am sorry for the trouble I've caused you," said the fish, "but I think the sea is a fine place to live. It is the only home I have ever known. However, your wife shall have a house of wood."

The fisherman was returning home, when his wife met him on the road. She had a rolling pin in her hand, and fire in her eyes.

"What is the matter now?" asked the fisherman.

"What's the matter?" snapped his wife. "Just you take a look."

The fisherman looked. He saw a gigantic wooden ark.

"We can't live in that," she snarled. "Get back to that fish. Tell him we want a large house of stone."

For the third time the man had an audience with the fish, and relayed his wife's decree.

"Your wife is very hard to please," said the fish. "I have given her the finest and largest wooden house I have ever seen. However, your wife shall have a house of stone."

Upon his return home, the fisherman saw the house his wife had been given. He saw his wife pulling out her hair, jumping around, and screaming. He saw her pick up a large rock and come at him, snarling. He beat a hasty retreat back to the fish.

"No need to tell me," said the fish, "your wife is still unsatisfied. I gave her one of the finest houses the city of Atlantis has to offer. I can do no more for her."

"Oh, please, kind fish," said the fisherman, "please grant me one last wish. I have always been a poor fisherman. I do not have much to speak of. Now, I do not even have my wife, for she has turned against me. I fear my life is not worth much if I return home. Truth be told, I always feel happiest and at home when I'm on the sea. Therefore, I beg you; turn me into a fish, so that I might forever swim in its blue-green waters."

In an instant, the fisherman is transformed into a great fish. Leaping from the boat, he splashes into a new and wonderful life. ≡

Fool's Gold

A young man manages to gain an apprenticeship with a wizard, by feigning an interest in the arcane arts. His real purpose however, is to find out the wizard's secrets and then use them to make himself filthy rich.

The apprentice soon finds out that the wizard is slow in divulging his secrets, and so spends two years cleaning floors and dusting off the wizard's massive tomes. Every now and again, when he thinks the wizard is not looking, the apprentice opens the mammoth books in hopes of learning a spell or two. He is disturbed to find the books contain ancient scripts with which he is unfamiliar. Even more disturbing is that as he gazes upon the letters, they seem to writhe and twist like many snakes in a pit.

Finally the time comes when the wizard gives the apprentice a tour of a room, which holds magic gadgets and devices. "Harbor no ideas of making off with any of the items you see within this room," warns the wizard as they enter, "for they will bring you no profit."

The wizard's warning falls on deaf ears. The apprentice will not be denied a life of luxury, not after being the wizard's housemaid for so many years.

The apprentice asks questions of the wizard concerning the many things that clutter the room. He makes the questions sound innocent and casual, hoping not to convey his larcenous intent.

The wizard patiently answers the many questions. "That is a horn used to summon an invincible army. That is a mirror, which allows the person who gazes upon it, to see his future. Those two pieces of cloth may look identical, but one yields a never-ending supply of food, and one provides its bearer with a never-ending supply of gold." The wizard demonstrates the magic of the gold-producing cloth. He spreads it flat, and upon it appear thick medallions of gold.

"Huzzah!" thinks the apprentice, his heart thumping hard within his chest. "Jackpot!"

Later, when night falls, the apprentice creeps back to the magic room. He darts into its darkened interior, snatches up the cloth that makes gold appear, stuffs it under his tunic and, taking a horse from the stable rides swiftly from the wizard's lair.

The wizard, unseen by the apprentice, stands at a window and smiles sadly as he watches the horse and rider flee into the dark forest.

The apprentice is deep within the forest before he stops and dismounts his lathered, heaving horse. He is eager to test his gold-producing cloth. As he removes the cloth from its hiding place, the apprentice thinks of the many things he will purchase with his abundant wealth. The cloth is spread, and upon it appear thick medallions of bread, salami, a wedge of cheese, a bowl of cabbage soup, and a half-full wineskin.

The apprentice is flabbergasted. "How could I have chosen the wrong cloth?" he wails.

Unknown to the apprentice, the wizard had seen through his ploy and so switched the positions of the two cloths. The hapless apprentice unwittingly snatched up the culinary cloth. It is to be his only recompense for his years of service to the wizard.

Feeling utterly dejected, the apprentice remounts the horse. He plods through the forest for many weeks, unable to find his way to civilization. His magic cloth ensures he does not starve, but he has become tired of the plain fare the culinary cloth produces.

After six months of tramping through the forest, he comes across a wild-man. The wild-man is gaunt and filthy. A white mane of hair, and long white beard frame his bug-eyed, sunken-cheeked face. His clothing is in shreds, and there are no shoes on his thickly-callused feet.

The wild-man has sought the exit to this forest for many years, ever since he fled from the wizard's abode, taking with him certain magical items. "Stranger," says the wild-man in a voice grown raspy from disuse, "have you any food to spare?"

"Have I ever!" replies the apprentice ruefully. He spreads his culinary cloth and upon it appear thick medallions of bread, salami, a wedge of cheese, a bowl of cabbage soup, and a half-full wineskin.

The wild-man howls with excitement. He has survived for years on nuts, roots, berries, and what insects he managed to catch. So who can fault him for diving into the fare like the half-starved man he is? When at last he drains the last few drops from the wineskin, he looks at the apprentice. "Forgive me for being a glutton," he apologizes, "but it has been a very long time since I have tasted such delicious food."

"Make no apologies," replies the apprentice, "for there is more where that came from." He shakes the remnants from the cloth, folds it up, and then spreads it out on the ground. A moment later, upon it appears thick medallions of bread, salami, a wedge of cheese, a bowl of cabbage soup, and a half-full wineskin.

The wild-man claps his hands, rolls onto his back, and kicks up his heels in delight at the appearance of the food. Then he pounces upon the victuals as though he had not just eaten. After licking the bowl that once held cabbage soup, the wild-man leans back and belches mightily. He asks the apprentice how he has come to possess such a wonderful cloth.

The apprentice explains that it is an acquisition once owned by a wizard.

"I too have a few items once owned by a wizard," the wild-man says. "Would you be willing to trade?" As he speaks the wild-man brings into view a small box. He flashes a smile of yellowed and rotting teeth, and then he opens the box to reveal thick medallions of solid gold.

The apprentice is visibly shaken, and drools at the sight of the gold.

The wild-man dumps the medallions from the box, closes its lid, and then opens it again. The box is once again brimming with golden medallions.

The apprentice in his excitement almost loses his self-control.

"The cloth and your horse for this box," says the wild-man.

The apprentice readily agrees. The wild-man swipes up the cloth, scrambles onto the horse, and races away while cackling loudly.

The apprentice is left holding the box. He does not even notice the wild-man's departure. For over and over again he opens the box's lid, dumps the gold, and closes the lid. Before long he has amassed a large mound of golden medallions.

His stomach grumbles, and he instinctively reaches for the culinary-cloth. But it is not in its usual place. He looks for his horse, but that too is gone. Then he remembers the exchange he has made with the wild-man. He looks at the gold and hugs it close. He cannot leave it and go in search of food, for someone may come along and steal his gold. He has no way of carrying it away, and he dare not hide it lest he forget its whereabouts. The apprentice resolves to stay with his gold until food, or someone with food, comes to him. So he waits.

In time someone does indeed find him. It is the wild-man. In his haste to quit the forest, he had ridden feverishly until knocked from his speeding horse by an unseen tree branch. Battered and bruised, he had watched helplessly as the horse galloped away. The wild-man has employed the services of the culinary cloth so frequently, that it is now too tattered to work properly.

He now looks down at the bones of the apprentice; they are draped across a mound of gold. The wild-man shakes his head pityingly. "We were fools to think that we could outwit the wizard," he laments. "It is too bad, lad, that you and I learned too late that the wizard's box only contains fool's gold." Leaving the gold and magic box where they lay, the wild-man continues his search for the exit to an endless forest. ≡

Help Comes to the Homestead

There once was a poor young man who, from day to day, eked out a living on his small homestead.

One day a young maiden and old woman happen by. The maiden tells the young man they are lost and tired. She goes on to say she will gladly do chores in exchange for food and lodging.

The young man agrees to the maiden's terms. He could use the help.

They share a meal of gruel and bread and then turn in for the night.

The next morning, the maiden insists on milking the cow. Her clumsy and inefficient milking technique leaves the cow's teats irritated and chafed. What little milk she manages to get anoints the parched earth as she knocks over the milking bucket.

The young man is sorry there will be no milk for his breakfast, but his kind nature prohibits reproof against the maiden. He will content himself with a couple of fried eggs.

At this very moment the maiden is collecting the eggs from the chicken coop. You can tell that she is not used to dealing with chickens. Just look at how she leaves the door to the coop wide open. The chickens take this as an open invitation to fly the coop.

The maiden tries to retrieve the fowl, but with her apron full of eggs it is very awkward to do. The only thing she manages is to trip and land heavily on the eggs. It looks as though the young man will have to go this day without eggs as well as milk.

The young man takes the crushed eggs in stride and settles for a few crusts of stale bread for his breakfast. After washing down his breakfast with a flagon of tepid water, he announces his intention of doing his laundry at the river.

"Oh," says the maiden, "as my apron is now in need of a wash, please allow me to launder your shirt as well."

The young man relinquishes his shirt to the maiden for washing.

With lightness in her step, the maiden goes to the river. She is in the process of washing the young man's shirt, when she is distracted by all of the beautiful flowers growing nearby. She envisions a bouquet of them looking lovely on the kitchen table, and so commences to gather them.

While she is busy picking posies, the young man's shirt floats away down the river. After a time, the maiden returns to the river clutching a fistful of flowers. She is thunderstruck to see that the shirt she had been washing is missing. She surmises that in her absence, the river washed it away.

With a tear in her eye, the maiden tells the young man the shirt tale. The young man is dismayed upon hearing of the loss of his shirt. It was the only shirt he possessed. However, there is nothing that can be done. He tells the maiden not to worry, and that he can make do without a shirt.

The young man decides to do some work in his garden.

"While he is out," says the maiden to the old woman, "I will bake him some loaves of bread." So the maiden gathers together a few ingredients, kneads them, and then she fashions them into loaves. She then puts the loaves into a very hot oven to bake.

While the loaves are baking, the maiden takes a walk and explores the homestead. She comes upon a rabbit hutch. The rabbits look so cute and cuddly that she cannot resist opening the hutch to pet them. The moment she unlatches the door the rabbits leap out and head for the garden. They hop here and there devouring as much of the garden produce as they can. They have had their eyes on this garden for a long time. It is a rabbit's paradise.

The young man's attempts to rally the rabbits are futile. In short order his garden is a shambles. Whatever shall he do?

He needs these crops to see him through the winter. It is too late in the season to re-seed. He won't even have rabbit meat to sustain him through those lean months. For the rabbits, having sated their appetites, are escaping by squeezing through the hedgerow. How could things get any worse, wonders the young man?

The answer comes in the form of smoke billowing from the roof of his home. The bread in the oven has caught fire and the fire is spreading throughout the house. Buckets of water are thrown onto the flames, but have little effect. The fire rages on. In the end, nothing is left except smoldering timbers.

The young man sits slumped on a stump regarding what remains of his house. He is hungry, half dressed, and covered in soot. Yet, even after all of this, he does not rebuke the maiden.

Just then the old woman lays a hand on the young man's shoulder. "My dear young man" she says in a voice that resounds with youth, "you possess a kind and patient heart. Such qualities are rare in this world."

The young man turns to see not the old woman of before, but a beautiful lady shimmering in emerald green.

"I am the queen of the forest," she continues. "One of my daughters has taken a fancy to you and desires to be your wife. It is my experience that men can be greedy and wicked of heart. So before I would give my daughter my blessing I had to first test you. You have indeed passed the test. Do not fret over what has been lost, for your lot in life shall be much greater than it was before."

As the queen finishes these words, there appear buildings of majesty and the land is thickly covered in fine, healthy crops.

The maiden steps forward shyly. She is now dressed in a beautiful, green gown. There are flowers in her hair. It is a sight which makes the young man weak in the knees.

There is no question that they will live happily ever after, and so they do. ≡

Landers and the Golden Key

$\mathcal{L}$anders is traveling through a province that is unfamiliar to him, when he sees a stone tower. In the tower's upper most window, a veiled maiden gazes over the countryside. As this is the first person Landers has seen for many miles, he decides to go and speak with her.

Landers stands under the window and shouts a greeting to the maiden. She shouts a greeting in return.

"My neck is sure to get quite sore and stiff if I must converse with you from yon window," says Landers. "Please come down," continues Landers, gesturing to the door in front of him, "so that we may talk more comfortably."

"I cannot," replies the maiden, "for that door has been locked for many years. Only a special golden key will unlock the door. If you would have the key, you must seek out the wise and mystic tortoise that dwells in the distant northern forest. He can tell you where the key may be found."

"Then I shall seek out this mystic tortoise," says Landers. "I will acquire the golden key and use it to open this door that has been for so many years locked. Before I start on my quest, please let me gaze upon your face. I will hold your lovely image in my mind as I trek."

"I dare not!" says the maiden. "This is our first meeting, and I am terribly shy. But please take this with you for your journey. It is a meal that I have prepared with my own hands." She drops a bundle to Landers.

"I am off then," shouts Landers, "fear not, I shall return with the key." Off he goes.

It isn't long before the scrumptious aroma emanating from the bundled food, has Landers salivating. He unties the bundle and digs in. "What an exceptional cook this maiden is!" says Landers around a mouthful of quiche. After licking his fingers, he continues his journey.

Landers travels for a long time before entering the forest where he is to seek the tortoise. He is tired, famished, and wishing that he had not eaten all of his food so early into his journey. He wanders through the forest for hours, before finding fallen nuts at the base of a tree. Landers snatches up a handful of nuts and a rock. He begins to feverishly crack the nuts against a small boulder.

"Son," says a weary voice, "will you kindly stop cracking nuts on my shell?"

Landers drops the rock and scrambles back like a crab. He spends some silent moments peering at the object he has mistaken for a small boulder. "Are you the mystic tortoise?" asks Landers, hesitantly.

"Yes," replies the tortoise, "I am a tortoise. Though I am no mystic."

"I apologize for shattering nuts on your shell, but I thought you were just an old boulder," says Landers.

"Just an old boulder?" says the tortoise, indignantly. "Why, there was a time when I was the grandest tortoise in the land. That was before I became covered with lichen, mushrooms, and other vegetation. What is your reason for coming here? Is there something you want of me?"

"Indeed there is," returns Landers. "I am told that you know where I might find the golden key that will free the maiden from her confinement in the tower."

"Golden key?" asks the tortoise. "Hmm...I vaguely remember something about a key, and I think it may have been a golden one at that. But, of course, that was a long time ago, and my memory is not what it used to be. All I've been able to think about these past years is the sorry state my shell is in. Perhaps if you were to clean it up for me, my mind would be free to think of other things, like the golden key you seek."

Landers sets to work cleaning the tortoise's shell. It is a difficult task, for he has not the proper tools for such labor. Eventually, after much scraping and buffing, the tortoise's shell gleams.

The tortoise is very happy as he cranes his neck to inspect his shell. "Nice work, lad!" he exclaims. "Now it occurs to me that you must seek out the mountain lion that lives in the mountains to the east. He shall know the whereabouts of the golden key."

Landers thanks the tortoise and heads east towards the distant mountain peaks. After days of walking, he finally reaches the foot of the mountain. His heart sinks, for the mountainside seems impossible to climb. But he must not fail the maiden in the tower. Mustering his courage, he begins his ascent. He climbs carefully, groping for hand and footholds. Several times rocks crumble beneath his touch, and each time he manages to save himself.

Every muscle in his body is red-hot with pain by the time Landers heaves himself over the top of the rock face. He lies for some time on the soft grass, gasping for air. Soon he is beset by an overwhelming desire for food and water. Pushing himself to his feet, he staggers off in search of both.

After a brief search he finds a patch of blackberries. He pounces on them hungrily, ignoring the needle-sharp thorns pricking his flesh. He picks as many berries as he can reach without falling headlong into the thorny patch. Taking a handful of the berries, he perches on a rock to eat. He smacks his lips with delight, for the blackberries are juicy and delicious. His repast is interrupted by a deep, gravelly voice.

"Is that the sound of someone eating?" booms the unseen speaker. "Is someone eating something juicy and delicious?"

Landers wants to run but his feet seem to be rooted to the ground. His bones turn to water and he collapses into an unconscious heap when a gigantic mountain lion drags its bulk into view.

When Landers regains consciousness, he finds the mountain lion watching him intently. Landers manages to ask, "Are you the mountain lion of which the mystic tortoise spoke? He says that you can tell me the location of the golden key that will free the maiden from the tower."

The mountain lion continues to study Landers for a moment, before answering. "Golden key?" asks the lion. "Hmm...I vaguely remember something about a golden key, but that was ages ago. My memory is not what it used to be, ever since my joints became so stiff and painful that I can no longer hunt. Hunger so occupies my mind that I can scarcely think of anything else. If you were to bring me something to eat, my mind would be free to think of other things, like the golden key which you seek."

Landers fashions for himself a sling and a bow with arrows, then he goes hunting. It takes him a very long time to acquire enough food to satisfy the mammoth mountain lion's appetite. Eventually, the lion burps with satisfaction and says to Landers, "You must seek out the ancient fish that dwells in the valley. He can tell you of the place where the golden key may be found."

Landers has no choice but to turn his steps towards the valley. Getting into the valley is no easy jaunt. Landers must hold onto the trees as he descends, for he might lose his footing and crack his skull.

He is battered and tattered upon reaching the valley. He is near the limit of his endurance and must have water and sleep. He comes across a body of water and drinks deeply. The water tastes slightly brackish but it is welcome. He submerges himself to his chin, and the cool water dulls the pain in his muscles. Tired and achy he may be, but he leaps from the water when he hears, "It has been a long time since I have had a visitor."

Landers looks upon the largest fish he has ever seen. "Y-you must b-be the ancient f-fish," stammers Landers, in awe.

"Yes, it is true," replies the fish, "I am quite old."

"The lion in the mountains says you can tell me where to find the golden key that will free the maiden from the tower," reports Landers.

"Golden key?" asks the fish. "Hmm…I seem to vaguely recall something about a golden key. However, that was a long, long time ago. My memory is not what it used to be, ever since the water in which I live has become dangerously low. That I will soon be high and dry is all I can think about. If you were to dig a ditch down to the lake below, this water would wash me down into the lake. My mind would then be free to think of other things, like the whereabouts of the golden key."

Landers begins the backbreaking task of digging a ditch to the lake. His labors seem endless, but he eventually finishes. He opens the way for the fish, and the water sweeps it into the lake.

The fish is very pleased. "You will find the golden key," says the fish, "in the bottom of the pond from which you have freed me. Good luck to you!" And with those parting words the fish disappears beneath the water's surface.

Landers retrieves the golden key and hastens back to the tower. When he reaches the tower he turns the key in the lock, and then triumphantly opens the door. The veiled maiden steps out.

Her veil falls away and Landers marvels at her beauty.

"Now, my lady," says Landers victoriously, "you are free of your prison."

"Prison?" inquires the maiden. "This is no prison, this is my home and I have no intention of leaving it."

"B-but...the golden key?" says a confused Landers. "I thought—."

"All I said," interrupts the maiden, "was that this door was locked and if you wished to open it you must seek out the wise and mystic tortoise. However, the backdoor is not locked and I can come and go as I please."

This news is too much for Landers and he faints dead away. When he regains his wits, the maiden invites him in to tea. Over tea and biscuits, Landers learns that the maiden's name is Rose. He tells Rose of his trials in acquiring the golden key.

Rose is deeply touched by the hardships Landers bore in order to aid her, though she had no need of aid. It shows that he is of good character. She asks Landers if he would mind helping her make some much-needed repairs on the tower.

Landers is more than happy to help with the repairs, over the course of which he and Rose fall deeply in love.

Who would have thought that the golden key would not only serve as a key to the front door of the tower, but also a key to a deep and lasting love? ≡

The Lion and the Pig

A lion will usually give up a chase, if a few all-out bursts of speed fail to land it its prey. So it is strange that a lion, huffing and wheezing, is approaching the limits of his endurance, having pursued a pig for the better part of an hour. Or is it strange?

This particular lion is quite old. His hunting skills have declined and so has his strength. Long stretches without food, have caused his rib bones to become prominent features on his once meaty and powerful frame.

How then could the lion resist leaping after the plump, succulent, dimwitted pig that had stumbled across his path? However, what should have been a short sprint to a ham dinner has turned into a marathon. The lion invests every last ounce of his strength and endurance into this chase.

The pig has not survived his many years by being slow of hoof, or slack of wit. He races away from the lion, fueled by the thought of what his fate could be if the lion should make his acquaintance. The pig imagines that he can feel the lion's hot breath upon his neck, and the pig digs even deeper into his energy reserves.

Presently, there sounds a loud crash, a mighty roar of rage, and then a mewling of anguish and frustration. The pig continues his flight, but upon hearing no sounds of pursuit, he slows to a cautious trot, and then halts.

Has the lion given up the chase? Curiosity causes the pig to investigate. What the pig finds is the lion tangled in a hunter's net.

The lion looks at the pig through frenzied eyes, its sides heaving like a bellows.

The pig, seeing that he no longer need fear the lion, turns to leave.

"Wait!" says the lion. "Surely you will not leave me here to be a trophy for the huntsmen?"

"What should I do then," asks the pig, "set you free that you may fall upon me? I am not so dimwitted as you may think!" The pig turns to leave.

"WAIT!" calls the lion, his panic rising. "I promise not to harm you, if you will just free me. In truth, I find that I no longer have a taste for meat. Get me out of this trap, and I shall be an herbivore from this day forward, only eating such soups and broths that contain no meat. And you and I can be life-long companions."

The pig contemplates the lion's offer. "So, if I free you no harm will befall me?" asks the pig. "And we shall be friends for life? I have your word as the King of Beasts?"

"You have my word," says the lion, with a toothy grin, "as the King of Beasts."

"One moment then," says the pig. He turns and retreats into the surrounding growth.

As the minutes lapse, the lion wonders if the pig has abandoned him. However, with a rustle of leaves, the pig reappears. The lion opens his mouth to voice his relief at seeing the pig again, and the pig tosses a small green packet into the lion's opened mouth.

"Gack!" says the lion, almost choking on the pig's proffering. "Hey! Are you trying to finish me?"

"Oh no," replies the pig. "It is just a little something to aid you in keeping your promise."

Upon a sudden, the lion feels extremely drowsy. Soon he is in a deep sleep. He burbles softly, as the pig extracts him from the net.

After a time, the lion awakens. He is safe within the home of the pig. With bleary eyes he surveys his surroundings. His stomach grumbles, and hunger assails him.

"You have extracted me from the trap," says the lion, his yellow eyes full of malevolence. "I owe you my deepest gratitude. Come closer, so that I may shank you properly."

"Shank me?" asks the pig in surprise.

"No," replies the lion, shaking his great mane from side to side. "I want to shank y—." The lion cuts his words short, and a tremor of dread rushes through him. He runs his rough tongue along the inside of his mouth, and is flabbergasted. He hangs his head low, utterly defeated. For during his slumber, the pig had extracted him from the huntsmen's trap, but fearing the lion's trap, had extracted all of the lion's teeth. As an added precaution, the pig has also removed the lion's claws.

"You can shank me later," says the pig with a smile. "For now, you must be quite hungry. Come. Let us eat. I have prepared a hearty broth that is sure to hit the spot."

The lion resigns to his fate. He seats himself, and begins lapping steaming broth into his toothless maw. The lion pauses, looking up to give the pig a gummy grin.

"You," says the lion, "are quite a cook!"

The pig smiles and snorts in appreciation.

And so it is, that through a strange turn of events, a lion and a pig live companionably for the rest of their days. ≡

The Lion and the Pig

The Magic Genie

𝔐ae thinks the violin is the most wonderful musical instrument in the whole world. On Saturdays, she goes to the library and spends hours listening to the library's large collection of music, featuring the violin.

"Oh, what sweet music!" Mae breathes. "If only I could play like the great musicians I hear, how happy I would be!"

The lights in the library flick on and off three times. It is a signal that the library is closing for the day.

Mae does not notice, for she has her eyes closed and is enthralled by the music she hears.

The door to the listening room opens, and a librarian steps in. The librarians are always sure to check every room before locking the doors. Especially the listening room, for within it they usually find Mae in a hypnotic state, from which she must be roused. It happens every Saturday and they are used to it. "Mae," says the librarian, while gently prodding Mae's shoulder. "I'm sorry, dear, but it's closing time."

Mae sighs deeply, reluctantly heaves herself out of her chair, and heads for the exit.

As Mae makes her way home, she daydreams of being a great violin player.

The darkening sky and a peal of thunder snaps Mae out of her daydream. A storm is brewing. The wind catches Mae and propels her forward, helping her reach more quickly the stretch of beach that leads to her house. Mae marvels at the power of the ocean waves as they pound the shore.

It is fortunate that the house, in which Mae and her family live, is a safe enough distance from the waters so as not to be washed away.

Mae eats, washes, and goes to bed. The storm rages on.

Come the dawn, Mae runs along the beach looking at and picking up things that have washed ashore. She notices sunlight gleaming on an object in the distance. She runs to it and is surprised to see that it's an old oil lamp. She brushes off the sand, and "POOF", before her stands a genie.

Mae is astonished by the appearance of the genie, so much so that she drops the lamp and turns to flee.

"Please, little one," says the genie in a gentle voice, "do not be afraid. I shall not harm you. I am the genie of the lamp. For 5000 years I have been confined to its cramped quarters. By rubbing the lamp you have freed me, and I am grateful. To show my gratitude I shall grant you one wish."

Without hesitation, Mae wishes to be a great violin player.

"Your wish," says the genie with a grand flourish, "shall be granted."

Mae is overjoyed.

Mae and the genie stand looking at each other. When after a few moments nothing seems to have changed, Mae inquires, "Where is my violin?"

"Violin?" inquires the genie. "You did not wish for a violin."

"Well, how can I be a great violinist without a violin?" asks Mae.

"Do not worry," says the genie, "you shall have one. We need only go to he that sells instruments, and buy one."

"Can't I just wish for one?" questions Mae.

"Sorry," reports the genie, "but you have used up your one wish already."

Mae and the genie go in search of a music merchant. They find one in town. Looking through the store window, they spy a violin. It has a price tag of fifty dollars.

"I wish I had fifty dollars," sighs Mae.

"You have already had your one wish," repeats the genie, "but acquiring sufficient funds will be easy."

Mae finally accumulates fifty dollars, and she rushes to buy the violin. It is a lovely instrument. She can hardly wait to hear the sweet notes she will play.

After carefully stringing the bow, Mae takes the violin from its case. She places it under her chin and gently moves the bow across the strings. All she can manage are a few squeaks and squawks. She is very disappointed.

"I thought you said I would be a great violin player?" laments Mae.

"And so you shall," promises the genie. He hands Mae a piece of sheet music.

"I can't read music," moans Mae.

"Ah!" says the genie excitedly, "Then you must learn."

So Mae practices hard everyday. Each day she gets better and better. Many months pass, and friends and family marvel at the beautiful music she produces as if by magic.

Eventually, Mae plays to a packed house at Carnegie Hall. Her wish has finally come true, due to the mystic powers of the magic genie. Right? ≡

The Magic Genie

Noisome Nelson

Nelson is a young man who attracts the attention of young maidens wherever he goes. This proves to be detrimental for Nelson, for one day he attracts the attention of a sorceress.

Nelson, who is also a good judge of character, sees the sorceress for the wicked person that she is, and refuses to give her the time of day. This infuriates the sorceress, and in a jealous rage, she places a powerful curse upon Nelson.

The curse causes Nelson to smell like a combination of meat rotting in the sun and an overflowing outhouse. Along with the overwhelming stench, comes invincibility. Nothing can harm Nelson, and he will never grow old. The sorceress wants to be sure that Nelson will forever walk the earth, suffering under the curse.

The curse yields immediate results, for every living creature flees in the face of Nelson's coming. Nelson is without companionship, and so it will be as long as he is enshrouded in a stinking miasma.

Nelson wanders aimlessly until he finds himself in a land where a ruler, known as King Phifer, has had his castle overthrown by brigands.

The brigands have ousted the king and his family. This has prompted the king to offer half of his kingdom and his eldest daughter's hand in marriage to anyone who removes the brigands from the castle.

The brigands are a mean and nasty lot and, so far, no one has been willing to risk his neck for the king. Even the offer of the king's eldest daughter and half a kingdom has not been lure enough.

Nelson, upon learning of the king's offer, tells the king that the castle will be empty by morning.

The king is glad to hear this news, but almost meets his end by way of Nelson's stench.

Only the king's youngest daughter is unaffected by Nelson's odious emanation. And that is because she has a terrible head cold and, therefore, can smell nothing. She even shows Nelson a kindness by offering him something to eat and drink. However, through hand signals, the king assures his daughter that Nelson must be anxious to complete his task.

Indeed, Nelson is anxious to meet with the brigands. He thanks the king's daughter for her kindness, and heads for the castle. Under cover of darkness, Nelson sneaks unseen into the castle. It takes but a moment for Nelson's nauseating stench to waft throughout the halls and chambers of the castle.

The brigands, gasping for air, race from the castle and are probably still running to this day.

By morning, the castle has aired out and the king moves back in. The king is pleased to once again sit upon his favorite chair in the throne room. Now that things are back to normal, the king has second thoughts about giving up half of his kingdom. He conveniently forgets his promise to give Nelson half of his kingdom and his eldest daughter in marriage. Everyone in the king's court assures the king that they, too, have no recollection of any such promises. So when Nelson arrives to claim his due, he is greeted with hostility.

The castle's drawbridge is raised and archers line the castle's crenellations. At the king's command, the archers loose their arrows. The awful smell of Nelson's person makes the archers tremble so violently, that most of their arrows go awry. Any arrow that does find its intended target bounces off harmlessly. Remember the wicked spell has made Nelson impervious to harm.

The king tries everything to get rid of Nelson, but all of his attempts meet with failure. Weapons are useless against Nelson, and Nelson is too clever to fall for any of the king's traps.

The people within the castle become uneasy and fearful of Nelson; they believe him to be a powerful wizard. They are also ashamed that their king would go back on the promise he made to Nelson. They overthrow the king and exile him from the castle.

Nelson receives half of the kingdom and the king's eldest daughter to wed. The eldest daughter is horrified at the prospect of having to marry Nelson. She hires a band of stouthearted cutthroats.

The cutthroats are directed to capture Nelson, take him to a far-off land, and throw him into a volcano. The cutthroats do their job well, and poor Nelson is soon languishing in lava.

When the king's eldest daughter hears of Nelson's plunge, she is overjoyed. For she is sure that there is no way Nelson could survive the molten rock of the volcano.

The king moves back into his castle. He is just about to punish those who banished him, when Nelson walks into the castle's hall.

The eldest daughter is astonished to see that Nelson is still alive. Everyone is astonished to find that Nelson no longer smells like meat rotting in the sun and festering outhouses.

Yes, Nelson emerged from the lava unharmed. Though the volcano's lava has forever burned away the fetid fog that surrounded Nelson, he still retains his invincibility.

The king is once again banished from the castle. Nelson rules in his stead, and proves a wise and just king.

Nelson marries the former king's youngest daughter, who is now free of her head cold, and they live each day in happiness and love.

As for the former king, Phifer, he is still a ruler of land. But the land he now rules over is quite a bit smaller. ≡

The Peasant

*A*lone figure walks a dusty road. A gaunt and disheveled man dressed in the rags of a peasant. Although he is poor, he is a good and kind-hearted person. He has been out searching for work, without success.

Presently, he feels the earth tremble beneath his feet. Scarcely has he time to throw himself off the road when a speeding coach shoots by with a flurry of hooves.

Those within the coach laugh uproariously at the sight of the tumbling peasant.

The peasant is left choking on the billowing dust. He waits until the coach is out of sight before raising his fist above his head and shaking it in frustration. "The wealthy have no right to treat the poor so badly!" he says, angrily. "If they found themselves suddenly poor, they would see things differently." Having vented his anger, he continues on his way.

Rough treatment continues for the peasant when he reaches a town. In the market square, he offers to bend his back to any task in exchange for a meal. He has no takers, so must resort to extending an alms bowl. He hopes to get a few coins from a generous passerby.

A group of wealthy merchants, deep within a discussion about something or another, fail to see the peasant before they tread on him. Whether by design or accident, they crush his alms bowl underfoot.

When the peasant dares to offer comment on their blind clumsiness, he is paid in oaths, blows, and laughter.

He drags himself away, all the while wishing a pox upon the wealthy. "If they themselves were poor men such as I, they would see things differently!" murmurs the peasant, sulkily.

Overcome by the exhaustion of the day's events, he drops into a deep slumber.

The next morning the peasant lay for some time with his eyes still shut, for he imagines that he can feel wonderful warmth. He knows this cannot be true for he has spent the night under the stars and at this time of year the mornings are quite chilly. Beneath him the hard packed earth on which he has slept, now feels like the softest feather bed. He knows it is just a dream, and it is time he faced the reality of the day.

He opens his eyes and is immediately stunned. "I must have taken quite a hard blow to the head yesterday," says the peasant, "for my mind is playing tricks on me!"

The peasant lies in a canopied bed large enough to sleep four. The bed is situated in a richly decorated room. There is a large hearth in the room and in it, a fire crackles cheerfully.

By some enchantment, the peasant is now a very rich man. When he is convinced that all is not an illusion, he vows to do only good with his wealth. He will aid the poor and afflicted. He will be a shining example for others with wealth, nay all of humanity, to follow.

After finishing his five-course breakfast, he goes forth to earn his title as "Patron Saint to the Poor and Wretched". No deed goes undone if it will serve to ease the life of the suffering.

It isn't long before the news is far flung of a wealthy man who spreads his wealth among the unfortunate. In record time his estate is a campground for the homeless. They trample his flowers, bathe in his fountains, chop up his imported trees and shrubs to fuel their cook fires, and distribute their trash evenly throughout his grounds.

As the months wear on, the wealthy peasant develops a dislike for the poor; the stench that wafts into his home is almost unbearable. Soon he can stand it no longer.

He mounts a horse from one of his stables, and armed with a riding crop, goes forth to expel the vermin from his land. He charges into their midst, slashing the riding crop left and right.

The squatters flee before their benefactor turned madman. "Get packing, pestilence!" he yells.

In a few hours time, he has evicted the last of his guests. His efforts leave him sweating and heaving for breath. Wearily he directs his lathered mount towards the house. He dismounts and, dropping the horse's reins, plods into his bedchamber. He falls exhaustedly onto the bed and into slumber.

A cold blast of air awakens him. Without bothering to open his eyes, he calls for a house servant to come shut the window. No one answers his call. There is a rustling of some dry material and something flies into his face.

He jerks bolt upright, his eyes fly open, and he looks about wildly. He imagines the evicted have come back to exact revenge upon him. His vision clears and he sees the truth of his situation.

It is only fallen, dry leaves blown by the wind that have fueled his fear. Then he realizes with dismay that he is once again a peasant, with packed earth for his bed and the sky for his canopy. He is bemoaning the fickleness of fate, when the ground begins to tremble.

Scarcely has he time to throw himself to one side, when a group of wealthy horsemen rumble by. "Out of the way, knave!" they shout as they gallop past.

The peasant is left to cough and choke on billowing dust. He waits until the riders are out of sight, before rising to his feet. Dusting off his rags, he goes in search of work. He is poor, but he is a good, kind-hearted person, and he pities the wealthy. ≡

The Pharaoh's Prank

$\mathcal{T}$here was once a pharaoh, who loved to play practical and unpractical jokes. Wealth meant nothing to him, except that it allowed for more elaborate pranks and jokes. No one escaped being a victim of his mirth. People were filled with dread whenever they were summoned to one of his parties. They knew they would be the butt of his pranks, but they dare not refuse.

At his parties, the pharaoh would serve stones to his guests, cleverly painted to look like the most delicious and succulent of foods. Then he would bellow with laughter as his guests doggedly tried to gnaw the inedible fare.

Another time, he staged a large mock battle, in which the ships were secretly designed to become waterlogged and sink. The pharaoh shook with amusement as his sodden warriors splashed their way to shore.

One of the pharaoh's favorite pranks was to have chairs constructed so that they collapsed under the slightest weight.

A faulty bridge that broke asunder, when a certain number of people reached its midpoint, was another of the pharaoh's favorites.

The pharaoh thought all of this was great fun. He always had to have the last laugh.

He was in the process of putting the finishing touches on his greatest prank ever, when he died.

His pyramid completed, his sarcophagus was laid therein. Before the pyramid was sealed, a powerful wizard placed a secret spell within the pharaoh's inner chamber.

Time passed, and the desert sands covered all trace of the pyramid's existence. It was only by chance, that a fierce sandstorm uncovered the topmost portion of the structure. Eventually, it was found by an archaeologist who was searching for fame and fortune.

He poured his money into the excavation of the pyramid. He would accept no partners, the treasures he would find within, would be his alone. He shook uncontrollably in anticipation of the great wealth that would soon be his.

After spending the better part of a year digging away the sand, the entrance to the great pyramid was discovered. Above the door was a lintel that read, "A curse on all who enter here. Only misery and misfortune await you."

Superstitious nonsense, thought the archaeologist. He ordered his hired workers to break through the door. They bent their backs to the task, but their tools would barely etch the stone. More expensive tools were needed. It took years, and a great deal of the archaeologist's money, just to get through the front door.

Within the pyramid, there were many dead-end passages. These were meant to baffle grave robbers. The archaeologist was destined to find every dead-end passage the pyramid had to offer.

Doggedly he continued his search for the inner chamber. He believed the riches he would find would repay him many times over, for every expense and hardship. He would not be swayed from his goal.

Finally, his cash flow dried up. Once his money disappeared, so did his workforce.

He was left to persevere alone.

It took the archaeologist 40 years and every penny he could beg or borrow to continue the archaeological excavation. Blind passage after blind passage had driven him to the very brink of insanity. His clothes were mere rags. He was filthy. His mane of hair was a tangled, matted mess. His wild eyes were dark and sunken. But his heart was in his throat as the last blow was struck. The inner chamber had finally been breached.

He fell to his knees and scrambled through the opening. Soon he had a torch lit, and its golden glow filled the chamber.

The chamber was empty, except for a stone sarcophagus situated in the middle of the room. Moving closer the archaeologist noted an embossed depiction of a pharaoh.

With trembling and wizened hands, the archaeologist pried open the sarcophagus. There was a hissing sound as the vacuum seal was broken, and the ancient spell placed by the powerful wizard was activated. The lid snapped open and a grinning mask in the pharaoh's likeness sprang out. Startled, the archaeologist collapsed in a heap.

A moment later, mask and sarcophagus crumbled to dust. Hysterical laughter resounded throughout the chamber. It was the ancient spell wrought by the powerful wizard to ensure that, even thousands of years after his death, the pharaoh still got the last laugh. ≡

The Pharaoh's Prank

Poor Pernell

This is Pernell. He is a very poor man. He is also a very poor fisherman. For most of the day he sits patiently, waiting for a fish to bite. Finally, he gets a bite. It isn't a large fish, just enough for one meager meal. All the same, he is thankful for this minnow as he has not had anything to eat all day. His mouth waters as he imagines how tasty the fish will be. It would be nice if he had some butter to cook it with, but one cannot have everything, can they?

He gathers some twigs with which to make a fire for cooking. The fire is soon blazing and the fish sizzling on the end of a stick. The delicious aroma of cooking fish fills his nostrils. It is difficult for Pernell to be patient and allow the fish to cook thoroughly.

Just as he is about to remove the fish from the fire he notices someone standing by the edge of the woods, watching him. It is a little old man. This little man is gaunt, dirty, dressed in rags and looks as though he will topple over from hunger. He doesn't say a word; he just stares at Pernell.

Pernell beckons the little man to come and rest himself by the fire. Pernell offers the little man the steaming fish.

The little man thankfully accepts the offering without hesitation. He eats as one who has not tasted food for a long, long time. When he finishes his meal, he thanks Pernell again and totters off into the woods.

Pernell douses the fire and then, stomach rumbling, makes his way home.

The next day Pernell is again ready to try his luck at fishing. To his surprise, there is a new fishing pole in the place where his old one used to be. Taking up the new fishing pole, he heads to the lake. No sooner does he cast his hook into the water than he catches a fish. Pernell cannot believe his luck. He casts the line again. Once again, he immediately catches a big fat fish. This day, and every day after, Pernell will never be without a fat fish for his dinner.

Today Pernell needs to chop firewood. The snows will be coming soon, and there must be wood for the fireplace. Taking up his axe, he heads to the woods. The axe is not very sharp, so Pernell selects a tree that is not too big or tall. All day he hacks at the tree and makes progress very slowly. Finally as the sun is setting, he finishes his task. His muscles ache and his hands are swollen and bleeding. Just as the last of the firewood is put on his wagon, an old man happens by.

The old man eyes the wagonload of wood Pernell has exhausted himself chopping. The old man says that most nights he almost freezes to death from want of wood in his fireplace. He laments that at his age he is too old to swing an axe. He is sure he will not live to see spring but will freeze on some cold winter night.

114

Pernell gives the old man the load of wood, for surely Pernell would not want him to freeze to death.

The old man gratefully accepts Pernell's gift and promises to return Pernell's empty wagon on the morrow.

In his exhaustion, Pernell forgets to retrieve his axe from the wagon before the old man trundles off. Oh, well, Pernell is in no shape to chop more wood today anyway. He trudges home with a handful of twigs to burn against the nighttime chill.

In the morning, Pernell steps from his house to find his wagon already returned. It is empty except for a brand-new, shiny axe. Pernell takes the axe to the woods to try again to chop firewood. At the first swing the axe slices though the tree as though the tree were made of butter. Pernell is astounded. What a wondrous axe! In no time at all Pernell has a wagonload of wood, and heads home.

On his way home he sees something gleaming in the dirt. It is a gold sovereign. Some wealthy merchant must have dropped it during his travels, leaving it to be trod upon by horses and wagons. Pernell can't believe his luck. Never has he held so much money in his hand. Pernell puts it in his empty purse. He begins to imagine all of the things he will purchase with his newly-found wealth.

By chance he meets an old lady sitting on a decaying log, at the side of road. She is dressed in rags, coughing furiously, and looks in ill health.

Pernell inquires if he might be of help to her.

She replies that her health is failing. She says that she needs medicine from the merchant in town, but the medicine is wickedly expensive. She is penniless. If she cannot acquire the money for medicine soon she is surely headed for the bone yard.

Pernell retrieves the gold sovereign from his purse. He gives it to the ailing old woman and wishes her a speedy road to recovery.

With tears in her eyes, the old woman thanks him and she hobbles toward the town.

Pernell, his purse once again as empty as when the day started, sets off for home.

As he sits at his table eating his evening meal, he feels something thump inside his purse. Reaching within he pulls out a gold sovereign. He is so amazed that he almost falls from his chair. Presently, he feels another thump inside his purse. It is another gold sovereign. This continues throughout the night. By morning, there is a great pile of gold sovereigns on Pernell's table. Imagine this, a purse that gives an endless supply of gold. Pernell does not have to imagine, for he has it!

There is a knock at the door. Pernell opens it on a beautiful maiden. So beautiful is she, that the sight of her momentarily takes Pernell's breath away.

She tells him that she was the little old man to whom he had given fish, the old man to whom he had given wood, and the old woman to whom he had given his gold. With his generous acts of kindness, he has broken the spell placed upon her by a wicked witch. For only one pure of heart could free her.

Pernell is astonished by the maiden's tale. But it does not take him long to get over his shock. For soon they are married and live happily ever after. ≡

Silence is Golden

*J*oseph, a young man from a far away land, is traveling through a country village when he sees the most beautiful maiden he has ever set eyes upon. She is carrying pails of milk. Joseph introduces himself.

"Good day to you, fair maiden," says Joseph. "Are you carrying your milk to the market?"

The maiden does not answer. She gives Joseph a shy look, a fleeting smile, and continues on her way.

Joseph is looking after the maiden when a man comes up behind him.

"She's a real beauty, ain't she?" says the man. "The only problem is, she don't speak! Ain't said a word, nary a sound out of 'er from the day she was born. A strange lass that one is." Having had his say, the man goes about his business.

Joseph is in no way deterred by the maiden's inability to speak. He is love-struck and will not rest until she is his wife.

Joseph learns that the maiden's name is Maria, and the courting begins. After a long while, Joseph's patience and persistence pays off. The maiden agrees to be his wife.

They are deeply in love with each other and their life together is exceedingly happy.

The years go by and their love grows ever stronger. It remains strong through the good and lean times. The fact that Maria does not speak has been no hindrance at all.

One day Maria decides that she will attempt to tell Joseph in words, how much she loves and cherishes him. So that night, when they have almost finished eating dinner, she opens her mouth to speak. Instead of words tumbling out, a golden nugget falls out of her mouth and onto the table.

Joseph picks up the golden nugget and looks at it in wonder and confusion. He is not quite sure how the nugget managed to get into Maria's mouth.

When Maria again tries to speak, another golden nugget falls from her mouth. This continues for some time until there is a neat pile of golden nuggets on the dining table. Maria and Joseph are overjoyed.

Maria still wishes she could put into words the love she feels in her heart for Joseph, but the gold will allow them to make some much-needed repairs about the house.

Soon they have a much larger house than before, their stable is full of healthy livestock, and their land is thick with an assortment of crops. These are indeed the good times, and Joseph and Maria's love for each other grows even greater.

There comes a time when Joseph must take a trip to see about purchasing some cattle. He will not have to travel far, but he will be away for a few days.

While he is gone, a traveling mountebank meets Maria as she is returning home from shopping. He tries to converse with her, without success. When he discovers that she cannot speak, he offers her, for a small sum, a potion that will cure her.

Maria readily purchases the potion and swigs it quickly. She feels a burning sensation in her throat, and when it passes she finds that she can speak.

"Oh!" laughs Maria with excitement. "Won't Joseph be pleased? Now I can tell him what is in my heart!"

That evening Joseph returns home from his business trip. He and Maria sit down and have dinner as usual. When dinner is almost over Maria opens her mouth to speak. Instead of golden nuggets falling out, words spill out.

Joseph is so astonished that he leaps from his chair, and stares wide-eyed at Maria. He soon recovers from his initial shock and is overcome with joy.

Maria tells Joseph of the love that is in her heart for him. She does so at great length.

As the night wears on, Joseph loses his battle with drowsiness and falls asleep. When he awakens the next morning, Maria is still talking.

Maria continues to talk non-stop for months on end. She seems to be making up for all of the years that she has been silent.

Finally, Joseph says, "My dearest love, please tell me again of the traveling mountebank who gave you the wondrous potion."

Maria is only too happy to comply. She retells the story, careful to include even the minutest details such as the gravy stains on the mountebank's striped shirt.

It is not until the next morning, that Maria finishes her saga. Through it all Joseph has remained alert, etching every detail into his memory. Now, Joseph stands up, stretches, and goes outside.

Following him, Maria inquires, "Joseph, where are you off to?"

"I am off to find the mountebank," says Joseph, "the Good Samaritan whose potion has given you a voice." Joseph opens his tool shed and chooses a very stout cudgel from his collection of tools. He smacks the cudgel hard against his open palm. "I wish," continues Joseph, "to thank him properly for this wonderful deed he has done." ≡

Silence is Golden

TAILOR

The Tailor

*P*hilip has been a tailor in this town for almost three years now. He likes the town well enough, and he makes a decent living by hemming dresses, pants, and making shirts. However, what he really and desperately wants to be is a fashion designer. Most of the people in the town only want traditional and conservative clothing, not cutting-edge fashions.

At night, after Philip closes the shop, he spends many hours in the backroom of his tailor shop illustrating fashion designs. Sometimes he will even take those illustrations and actually make clothes from them. Of course, no one will ever see them, let alone wear them. Philip is very careful to keep his creations out of sight. But one day, he gets careless.

Business is usually not very brisk in Philip's tailor shop, and during the lulls between customers he will work on his fashion clothing. He is in the process of sewing together one of his creations, when the little bell on the front door tinkles. He has a customer. He pulls back the curtain that separates the customer service area from his workroom, and greets the customer.

Philip knows just about everyone in this small town, but standing before him is a lady he has not seen before.

"I would like to have some dresses made," she says.

"No problem at all, Miss," says Philip. "Just choose a style from this book and I will take your measurements." Philip slides a book towards her.

She leafs through the book, and says with exasperation, "Don't you have anything more modern, more...in vogue?"

"I am sorry," says Philip, "but these styles are what all of the people in the town wear."

She rolls her eyes to the ceiling, and then she notices that the curtain to the backroom is not quite pulled shut. She looks into the backroom and sees one of Philip's secret creations. Her eyes go wide with delight. "What is that you have in that backroom?" she accuses.

Philip quickly jumps to close the curtain. "It is nothing," he replies, "nothing at all. It's just something that I...uh...it's nothing. Really!"

The lady gives Philip a long, hard, and disbelieving look. Then she spins on her heel and exits the shop.

When she is gone Philip exhales forcefully. He must be more careful in the future.

But little does Philip know that his life is about to change forever.

The lady, after leaving the shop, rushes home and tells her four sisters what she has seen in the tailor's shop. To confirm her suspicions, she sneaks back to the tailor shop after closing time. Through a window, she sees Philip illustrating fashions and sewing them together. "What beautiful and innovative designs!" she whispers to herself. Already, an idea is formulating in her head.

The next day she returns to the tailor shop, during business hours. She is there on the pretext of having a skirt hemmed, and she casually says, "I have a bolt of beautiful, imported cloth at home. I'm sure you will just love it! It was terribly expensive, but as I have no use for it, you may have it if you like. Just drop by after you close for the day. Here is my address." She hands Philip a card, and before Philip can muster an excuse, the door is closing behind her.

Philip looks at the card he has been given. He cannot explain why but he has an uneasy feeling. However, the idea of getting a beautiful and expensive bolt of cloth for free is a strong lure. Philip closes early and heads to the address on the card.

Philip knocks on the door of the house, and the door is flung wide. The lady that gave him the card greets him.

"Oh, it is you, Mr. Tailor!" she says with excitement. "Please…come in."

"Uh, thank you. Actually…my name is Philip," says Philip.

"Yes…Philip. These are my sisters, Philip," she says, gesturing to four ladies sitting at a dining table. "We are all about to have something to eat. Would you like to join us?"

She seats Philip at the table. She tucks a napkin under his chin and before Philip can collect his wits, soup is being spooned into his mouth.

Philip is just about to comment on this odd behavior and the even odder taste of the soup, when he begins to feel light-headed. As Philip swoons, the last vision he sees is the five ladies looking at him intently.

When Philip awakens, he feels awful. He feels even worse, when he discovers that he is in shackles. "What is the meaning of this?" demands Philip, in a quavering voice.

"Aah, ha ha!" laughs the lady.

"You lied about the cloth!" accuses Philip. "You don't have any cloth, do you?"

"Oh, yes," she says smoothly, "I have cloth. I have plenty of cloth. And you will use it to make dresses for my sisters and me. I've seen what you are capable of. The dresses you create will allow us to corner the Witches Fashion Design market."

"Witches Fashion Design market?" asks a confused Philip. "You mean all of you are witches?"

"That's right," she answers, "and with your designs we will be the queens of witch fashions. So you will remain chained here churning out designs and clothing." The witch studies Philip for a moment. "What's the matter?" she snaps. "Why look so sad, isn't this what you have always wanted to do? Now you will not have to slink around at night in the backroom of your tailor shop to do it. Here you may indulge in your passion twenty-four hours a day!"

"Yes but—," begins Philip.

"But what?" the witch interrupts.

"It is not part of my passion," says Philip, "to be shackled to a desk, and forced to design clothing for a bunch of witches!"

"No matter," she says. "We will leave you now, so that you may work."

Philip sits for a long time staring at a blank sheet of paper and feeling sorry for himself. Then he decides that it will be good to finally have someone wear his clothing designs, even if they are witches. He begins to work.

Philip creates beautiful and innovative clothing, which sets the witches well on the way to achieving their goal. But, unknown to the witches, Philip has a goal of his own.

One night, while the witches are out for the evening, Philip, straining at the limit of his chain, is able to reach their books on spells. He leafs through the books until he finds what he is looking for, and then he feverishly sets to work at his design table.

Upon their return from their evening out, the witches look in on Philip. They are surprised to see that Philip has designed five corsets, one for each of them. The witches squeal with delight and immediately try the corsets on.

The witches are looking with satisfaction at their reflections in a mirror when the corsets begin to tighten. The witches become alarmed and try to remove the corsets but it is no use. The corsets are so tight now that the witches cannot breathe, but still the corsets tighten and tighten.

Just when the witches think that they are about to shake hands with the devil, five loud popping sounds are heard. The corsets immediately loosen and fall to the floor. Their task is complete. Unknown to the witches, Philip has placed an enchantment on the corsets. The enchantment enabled the corsets to squeeze all of the wickedness out of the witches. They are witches no more.

The sisters, now free of their corsets, free Philip of his shackles.

The five sisters become Philip's fashion models, and together they corner the fashion-design market. ≡

The Tailor

To Twist or Not To Twist

*A*n elderly shoemaker, who has worked alone for many years, decides to take on an apprentice. He hangs a "Help Wanted" sign in his shop window.

A young man named Baldric answers his advertisement. Baldric does not know the first thing about making shoes but he promises to work hard and learn quickly.

The shoemaker agrees to hire him. "I will hire you," says the shoemaker, "but you must promise never to open this door. For if you do, only abject misery and heartache will be your lot."

"No, sir! I mean yes, sir!" says Baldric, with resolve. "This door has a knob that my wrist shall never twist!"

As it turns out, Baldric is a very industrious worker. He seems to be imbued with an endless supply of energy.

The old shoemaker approves of Baldric's work ethic. Production is up and the shoe sales have greatly increased.

At the end of each workday, the two of them laugh and have a merry time as they partake in their evening meal.

The old man is a wellspring of wisdom and stories and Baldric never tires of listening to him.

Day after day, week after week, year after year, Baldric works in very close proximity to the door and never seems to give it a thought. However, one day, when he is carrying a heavy load of shoe leather, he brushes against the forbidden-door's knob. The doorknob rattles a bit, and Baldric looks at the door as if seeing it for the first time. A strange feeling washes over him, and his hand reaches out for the knob.

"Baldric!" booms the old shoemaker, as he enters the room. "I would like to introduce you to my granddaughter, Alexandria."

The old man's words release Baldric from his trance. He turns to gaze upon Alexandria, and his heart melts. Not even in his dreams could he find a more beautiful lady.

Alexandria glares at Baldric challengingly, as if to say, "If you would court me, you have your work cut out for you!"

It is indeed no easy task to win the hand of Alexandria. The emotional turmoil of the courtship leaves Baldric almost too exhausted to do his work in the shoe shop. Finally, the old man intervenes, and pleads with Alexandria to stop toying with Baldric's heart.

Alexandria ceases her games and she and Baldric exchange vows.

The years that follow are the happiest Baldric has ever known. He and Alexandria have lovely children that grow up obedient and studious.

One night, when Baldric is sitting with his family around the fireplace, he says to his wife, "I must go out this evening, but the errand I run will take me but a few moments." So saying, he dons his cloak and rushes to the shoe shop.

Once inside the shop, Baldric moves with purpose to the forbidden door. He seizes the knob in an iron grip and gives it a mighty twist. What happens next is too swift for Baldric to comprehend.

The door flies open; Baldric is blinded by a bright light; he is sucked through the door, and the door slams shut behind him.

When he is able to see things clearly, he sees that he is in a meadow filled with beautiful flowers. Their sweet aroma fills his nostrils. Presently, he can hear music and laughter. It grows closer. He sees lovely maidens laughing and frolicking merrily.

The maidens' merriment becomes infectious as they surround Baldric in dance. They take him by the hand, feed him grapes, and have him swill a strange but delicious-tasting elixir. The heady elixir clouds Baldric's memories of his past and in short order he abandons himself to the hypnotic music and dancing.

Baldric, who from exhaustion has fallen asleep, now awakens to find himself alone in the meadow. The door, by which he has entered this land, looms before him. He grips the knob and gives it a twist.

As before, the door flies open; he is blinded by a bright light; he is sucked through the door, and the door bangs shut behind him.

Even before his eyes clear, Baldric can feel the cold. It is a bone-numbing cold, the likes of which he has never before felt. When his eyes do clear, he sees white for miles around. Of a sudden, he notices something moving towards him. It is a curious polar bear.

The snow scrunches under Baldric's feet as he looks around frantically for the door. He must hurry, for the polar bear is uncomfortably close now. Baldric's hands are almost frozen, and it takes him several tries before he is able to grip the knob and twist it.

Baldric can almost feel the polar bear's hot breath upon him, when the door flies open. Baldric is blinded by a bright light; he is sucked through the door; and the door booms shut behind him.

When his eyes clear, Baldric finds himself on a barren landscape of endless sand dunes. The heat of the sun is intense and a torrid breeze stings his eyes. Hot tears run down his cheeks.

Baldric's tears are those of one who has learned too late, the price of his folly. He must pay the price for breaking his promise to never twist the knob of the forbidden door. Now he will spend his existence traveling from one strange land to another. He had everything; now he has nothing except his memories of loved ones and of a shoe shop, to which he shall never return. ≡

Water

$\mathcal{R}$oland is a young peasant who earns his living by the sweat of his brow. He never expects a handout from anyone; it is just as well, for it is unlikely that he will ever be offered one.

The day is a right scorcher, and Roland has been toiling in a bean field for the better part of the day with scarce a drop of water. In truth, Roland has an uncanny ability to go for long periods without drink of any kind. At a point when most men would keel over from thirst, Roland is quite comfortable and unaffected. However, today's heat has Roland perspiring so profusely that to any on-looker he looks on the verge of collapse.

And it happens that an occupant in a passing coach sees Roland at his toil. Roland's sweat-soaked form causes the occupant to halt the coach.

Roland turns from his labors when he hears the coach stopping. He knows the coach for one of the royal fleet. His eyes grow wide with astonishment when he sees the king's daughter step from the coach.

The princess, being unusually kindhearted, believes Roland is on the brink of dehydration. She bids her lady-in-waiting bring her a flagon. Into the empty vessel, the princess pours water from her private-traveling stores. Then, holding the bejeweled flagon with both hands, she turns toward Roland.

Roland doesn't know whether to run, bow, or drop to his knees. So he remains frozen in his upright position.

The princess makes her way through the bean field until she is standing before Roland. "Young man," she says to Roland, "if you work on such a hot day as this, you must ensure that you remain properly hydrated." She proffers the bejeweled flagon of water to the stunned Roland.

He takes it with both of his trembling hands. Drops of the cool liquid slosh from the vessel.

"Careful now," says the princess, laughingly, "don't spill it all."

Roland, staring as though addled of wits, only manages a nod.

The princess, not waiting for Roland to empty the flagon of its fluid, returns to her coach.

Roland watches the coach's progress until it is a speck on the horizon. Then he looks at the flagon as if seeing it for the first time. He is astounded. Roland is not used to such an act of kindness and from the princess no less. A happiness floods into him. "The princess is kindhearted as well as beautiful," says Roland to himself. "I am determined that some day she shall be my wife. First I must become a proper suitor and that takes money. I resolve not to drink one drop of this water until I have become wealthy. I shall wait to savor this cool, sweet, life-giving fluid poured for me by the beautiful princess." So, holding his hand over the flagon to keep the water from spilling, Roland sets off in search of wealth.

Wealth is not easy to find, as Roland soon learns. His rags have become more ragged and his prospects seem ever more dim.

Days later, Roland is stumbling across an uncharted portion of desert. His throat aches with thirst, but he staunchly refuses to drink the water contained within the flagon.

Exhaustion and dehydration have Roland feeling light-headed. He sits down with the intent of resting a short while before continuing his quest but, instead, sinks into unconsciousness. Upon regaining his consciousness, Roland decides that, though it pains him greatly, he must sip from the flagon lest he be unable to continue.

Roland retrieves the flagon. And just as he is about to drink a frog pokes its head out of the water.

"Gribit!" croaks the frog. "This is the best-tasting water it has been my pleasure to wallow in. Thank you!"

Roland is horrified. What is a frog doing in his precious flagon of water? Now the water is sullied and undrinkable. Alas, Roland shall never see the princess again, for he shall surely die of thirst in this desert. Roland stares at the frog for a moment, and then he decides that his mind is playing tricks on him. He lifts the flagon to his lips, but falters. "Are you a real frog," asks Roland, "or are you a figment of my imagination?"

"Gribit!" replies the frog. "No, I am not really a frog. I am really a wizard that looks like a frog."

Roland begins to feel light-headed again.

"You see," continues the frog-wizard, "I, gribit, had an argument with another wizard. He, gribit gribit, caught me off guard, turned me into a frog, and sent me to the middle of this, gribit, desert. In my froggy form, I must have water, gribit, in order to perform my magic. Even so, it will take me a few years to regain, gribit, enough of my powers to restore myself to human form. But tell me, lad, what are you doing in this, gribit, unforgiving place?"

Roland tells the frog-wizard of the princess and of his search for wealth.

"Gribit! In return for the delicious water you have brought me," says the frog-wizard, "I shall help you." The water has indeed given the frog-wizard back a good portion of his powers. With the wave of a webbed foot, a magnificent castle surrounded by fine crops appears. There is a beautiful, clear lake where swans swim and fish frolic.

Moreover, Roland is no longer dressed in rags, but royal finery complete with a crown.

As Roland gazes in wonder, the castle's drawbridge lowers and a group of soldiers march from the castle. Upon reaching Roland, the captain of the guard bows and says, "My Liege, what is thy command?"

Roland can hardly believe his good fortune. He thanks the frog-wizard profusely. Roland then requests a bucket of water, which he downs in a few gulps. Wiping his mouth he says to the captain, "Please bring me a swift horse." Roland's request is quickly granted, and he hastens to the princess.

When he again meets the princess, she offers him a bejeweled flagon of water, so that he might wash the travel-dust from his throat. Roland thanks her, and drinks it down straightaway. The water is cool, and sweet.

"I have seen you before," says the princess to Roland. "You are the young man I met in the bean field. It seems that you have done well for yourself since I last saw you."

"Yes," replies Roland, "and I have come to ask for your hand in marriage."

The princess blushes and smiles shyly, but within six months she and Roland are husband and wife.

They live in the castle given to Roland by the frog-wizard, where they are exceedingly happy ever more. ≡

Wharton the Ram

*T*his is Farmer Brown. Farmer Brown has a lot of work to do on his farm. So much work that Farmer Brown often feels overwhelmed by the sheer magnitude of it.

He also has a lot of farm animals. He must feed and tend them every day. All of the animals like Farmer Brown, but there is one who is especially fond of him. It is Wharton the ram.

Wharton is a peculiar ram. He follows Farmer Brown all around the farm. He sometimes wears clothing and walks upright on his hind legs. But perhaps the most peculiar thing about Wharton is that he can read.

Wharton loves to read books. Actually, he reads everything he can get his hoofs on. Farmer Brown gets books for Wharton, on many different subjects, from the local library. As you can imagine, Wharton is a very smart ram. He would read all day long if he were not trailing Farmer Brown.

One day, while shadowing Farmer Brown around the farm, Wharton hears the Farmer lamenting. "I have so many chores, day in and day out!" says Farmer Brown mournfully. " I wish someone would do 'em, then I could have some free time. Maybe go fishin'."

Wharton is sad that Farmer Brown is unhappy. But presently, Wharton gets an idea. He will endeavor to make things easier for Farmer Brown; give him some much-needed time off.

The next morning, Wharton is up before the rooster crows. Dressed in his overalls, he busies himself about the farm.

Wharton sheers the sheep, feeds and waters the animals, curries the horses, milks the cows, fixes the broken-down car, repairs the washing machine, makes a few modifications on the old tractor, plants and waters the crops, repairs the barn, and repairs the wire and wood fences.

When Farmer Brown sees his ram doing all of the chores, he is amazed and very pleased. He follows Wharton around all day. Finally, he realizes Wharton can handle the chores just fine. Maybe even a little better than he can himself.

Farmer Brown finally has time to go fishing, and so he does.

This arrangement continues for some time. Wharton loves every minute of it. Farmer Brown, however, becomes increasingly bored. He has nothing to do. He has too much free time. Besides, Wharton looks like he's having an awful lot of fun.

Finally, Farmer Brown can stand being idle no longer. He sheepishly asks Wharton if things can go back to the way they were.

Wharton agrees, and things go back to normal. Almost…

Wharton is grazing contentedly and reading a book. Then he overhears Mrs. Brown bemoan, "All of these chores day in; day out. I wish someone else would do them!" ≡

The Witch in the Woods

(Inspired by "Hansel and Gretel" by the Brothers Grimm)

In a small cottage at the edge of a forest, there lives a man and his two children. The children, a girl and boy, are very sweet and very well behaved. Search as you might, you may never find another two like them.

The children willingly toil alongside their father from dawn until dusk. They help him with various chores in and about the house, never letting him feel overwhelmed by the weight of work. They never press their father for things which he cannot afford. They may not have all of the things that other children have, but they are happy.

The father thinks the world of his children. He does his best to provide for them and keep them cheerful. He thinks the children will be even happier if they have a mother to grow up with. So with that thought in his mind, he begins courting the Widow Prim.

The Widow Prim is just that, prim and proper. She likes to have things in apple-pie order, and becomes enraged when they are not to her liking. Of course, the father doesn't know this and he hopes that soon they will exchange vows.

The father realizes that he must have more money if he is to take a wife. He has heard rumors about gold being found in the far-off mountains. He decides to try his hand at prospecting. For the time that he is away, the Widow Prim will look after the children.

After their father takes his leave, the Widow Prim turns into a tyrant. She orders the children about as though they are trained monkeys, tickling their backs with a switch if they move too slowly. She lifts not a hand to help in the daily chores. She gives the children nothing to eat, but demands that they forage in the forest for their own food. On cold nights, she makes the children sleep without blankets saying, "You children need to be prepared for the harsh conditions you will face in later life." Under the Widow Prim's tutelage, the children learn all about harsh conditions.

One day, when the children are enjoying a very rare break, they hear music coming from the forest. It is a flute being played so enchantingly, that the children cannot resist seeking out its source. Suddenly, their legs are no longer under their control, but are bewitched by the music's spell. Deeper and deeper they travel into the forest.

The music leads them to a house in a clearing. The front door gapes wide. Without hesitation the children enter, and the door slams shut behind them. Within the gloom of the room comes a silky and sinister voice.

"Aah, yesss, welcome children! Welcome!" cackles a wicked witch. The witch is exceedingly hideous. Her face is covered with boils and it has a greenish hue. Her hair is falling out and her arms and legs are covered in an angry red rash. Her disposition is quite sour. Her breath is none too sweet either.

"You must be famished after your journey," clucks the witch. "Why, you are nothing but skin and bones. Here, sit down and eat." As the witch says these words, she shoves bowls of odiferous stew towards them.

The children gag a little as they peer at the stew. The stew is a greasy mixture of unidentifiable ingredients. Bobbing on top of the stew is something that looks like an eyeball. The children glance at each other and push the bowls from them.

"What's the matter," asks the witch, "don't like it?"

The children shake their heads, no.

The witch prepares something else for them, but still they refuse to eat. She serves up several of her savory recipes, but it is useless. The children have become quite ill from the sights and smells of her culinary efforts.

Finally, the witch flies into a rage. "If you don't like what I put before you," she screams, "then you shall have nothing at all to eat!" She then puts them to work.

The witch is taken aback, when the children attack their labors with gusto and glee. She shivers when the boy begins to whistle a merry tune. "What strange children have I lured into my home?" murmurs the witch to herself.

Little does the witch know, that after being under the thumb of the Widow Prim, slaving for the wicked witch is like being on vacation.

There are periods when the witch must leave the house. She does so in order to gather ingredients for her potions and spells. Before leaving, the witch casts a barrier spell that surrounds the yard. The children cannot get past this barrier to escape.

While the witch is gone, the girl goes into the yard. She gathers dandelion leaves and flowers, young thistle leaves, mushrooms, and other vegetation. She takes these into the house and uses them to make a meal for herself and her brother. They eat heartily.

When the witch returns home, she sniffs the air. "What is that I smell?" demands the witch.

The children only give her blank stares.

The witch wrinkles her nose. In truth, the curious smell makes the witch salivate. In the ensuing silence her stomach grumbles with hunger. "Get to work!" orders the witch.

On another occasion when the witch returns from foraging, her house is again filled with a delicious aroma. The witch's mouth waters and her belly growls with hunger. She is angry that she cannot catch the children in the act of whatever they do to make the house smell so good. She decides to spy on them.

One day, the witch pretends to leave but doubles back. She catches the children just as they are about to eat.

"Ah, ha!" roars the witch as she throws the door wide. "So this is what you have been up to. Get back! Let me see!" What the witch sees are two plates of leafy greens and various mushrooms. "Why, this is muck for forest animals," sneers the witch. "My cooking isn't good enough for you but you will eat this? Get to work!"

The children busy themselves with their chores.

While they work, the witch aims to throw out their food. However, the delectable aromas wafting from the fare beckon her to try some. Before she can stop herself, she has devoured both helpings.

After this the witch indulges in many more meals prepared by the little girl. The witch shuns her usual fare of greasy stew. She finds that she no longer has the stomach for it. "Those children have cast a spell on me," grumbles the witch, "for I no longer care for meat."

In due course the children gain favor with the witch. She begins to spend more and more time with them. The children entertain her with little skits, and the witch tells them stories of when she was a child.

The little girl collects plants and roots from the wild and makes a salve to put on the witch's boils. In a short time the witch's complexion clears up.

Because the witch no longer eats eye of newt, her hair has ceased to fall out and even starts to grow back.

Now it can be seen that the witch is actually quite a comely lady.

Joy and laughter have become very common in the little house.

The witch ceases to use the barrier spell to keep the children from leaving while she is away. She finds that she no longer wants to keep the children against their will. That the children have chosen to stay with her for so long, truly warms her heart.

One day, the witch notices the children are looking gloomy. "What ever is the matter, dear children?" asks the witch.

"It is our father," says the girl. "It has been many years since we have seen him, and we miss him so. We worry that he may be ill and in need of us."

The witch knew that one day the children would want to return to their own abode. She will be sad to see them go. She offers to be their travel companion and see them safely home.

When the children arrive at their home they are in dismay, for they find it empty and boarded up. Their father is nowhere to be seen. They inquire of their father's whereabouts at a neighbor's house.

The children learn their father has spent years searching high and low for them. He comes back from time-to-time to find out if by chance they might have returned. As for the Widow Prim, she has married a traveling merchant.

The children are sorry to hear that they have caused their father so much grief. They reopen their house and await their father's return.

They haven't long to wait for their father meets a fellow villager who informs him his children have returned. The father can scarcely believe the news. With all of the speed he can muster, he heads home.

Once he is home, there is a tearful reunion. The children tell him of the Widow Prim's treatment, and of their time in the witch's house.

Their father informs them that they are now very rich, for he has struck a fat vein of gold in the mountains.

Everyone is happy, even the witch, for the children plead with her to stay with them, and so she does. In the course of time she becomes their stepmother. She showers them with love and kindness all of her days. ≡

The Wizard's Flute

*A*n evil wizard, lashing his horse furiously, rides from a town which for a year has been his home.

The people of the town have grown tired of the vile magic the wizard spawns. They have risen against him. With the aid of a good wizard, they aim to show the evil conjurer just how much his presence is appreciated.

Such sentiment has the evil wizard throwing caution to the wind in his rush to put the town behind him. He knows all too well what is in store for him, should the angry assemblage catch hold of his robe. And for all of his command over the dark arts, he is not sure that they will shield him against the torch-bearing mob.

He is also at the disadvantage of being without many of his magical items, things that might prove useful in his predicament. He was able to snatch only a few items from his lair.

Unnoticed by the wizard one of these items, a flute, jostles from his pocket and lands on the dusty road.

The next morning, a vagabond comes across the wizard's flute. He picks it up and brushes it off. Then he puts it to his lips and expels an experimental puff of air.

The sound that the flute produces is unlike anything the vagabond has ever heard. He propels a few more puffs that follow the first one. Then he puts the flute into his pocket, thinking that he might amuse himself with it from time-to-time. The vagabond continues his way along the road, so he does not see the snakes.

Thousands of snakes converge on the spot where the vagabond had played the flute, for the flute's song had summoned them.

They are the first of the many undesirables that the vagabond will, unwittingly, send for by way of the flute. In one place it is locusts, in another place crickets, still another place ravens and, most recently, rats.

These plagues are the topic of conversation on everyone's lips. None can fathom the reasons they occur.

Meanwhile, the evil wizard halts his mount at a roadside inn. He has ridden hard for several days, and hopes he has outdistanced the enraged townsfolk and the good wizard who aids them. Entering the inn, he buys a tankard of cider to wash travel-dust from his dry throat. The wizard seats himself in the darkest part of the room, and swills his cider while keeping an eye on the door.

It is while he is thus situated, that he overhears two of the inn's patrons discussing the recent plagues. His ears prick-up when he hears the words snakes, locusts, crickets, ravens, and rats. The wizard knows of an object that will bring plagues of that type into being. His flute! "But it cannot be my flute," muses the wizard, "for it is here in my pocket." The wizard pats his pocket and is alarmed to find it empty.

The wizard calms himself, with the knowledge that he can use his magic to ascertain the whereabouts of his flute.

He tracks down the vagabond and confronts him. "You have a flute," accuses the wizard.

"Yes," replies the vagabond, showing his questioner the instrument, "and it plays the weirdest-sounding music."

Before the wizard can stop the vagabond, the vagabond begins to play. The resonance of the flute causes the earth to split asunder. The vagabond immediately ceases to play, but it is too late. Terrible creatures issue from the rent in the earth's crust.

The creatures, hissing and slobbering green ichor, advance. The object of their desire is not the terrified vagabond, but the wizard. "Old acquaintances", describes the relationship the wizard and creatures share. Maybe a better description would be master and slaves. For years the wizard has taken delight in using the powers of the flute to summon and torture these creatures into doing his evil biddings. The creatures could do nothing against the wizard, as long as the wizard held the flute. However, this time the flute is not in the wizard's possession.

The once-mighty wizard is now a pitiful sight to behold. As the creatures lay twisted hands on him, he screams, writhes, and protests. His exertions are fruitless, for the creatures take him.

The last of the creatures, before entering the abyss, turns to the vagabond and glares. "Human," says the creature, in a deep voice never meant for human ears, "if you would not someday share the fate of the wizard, get rid of the flute. Gather as many sticks as you can and burn the flute on a pyre. It will be wise to stay and make sure the flute has been totally destroyed."

The vagabond, who has been as a statue throughout the whole phenomenon, manages a twitch of a nod.

And with that, the last creature leaps into the crevice and the earth slams shut.

The vagabond is shaken into motion. He runs here and there gathering as many sticks as he can find. When a huge pile is accumulated, he tosses the flute on top, and sets fire to the heap. Within moments the seasoned sticks are blazing high. The vagabond seats himself a safe distance from the inferno. He will not leave until he is certain the flute is no more.

It is a long time before the smoldering mound is cool enough for an inspection. Braving the hot ash, the vagabond searches for any remnants of the flute. He sees none. Wanting to make absolutely certain, he stirs up the ash. The vagabond sucks in a quick breath when he uncovers gold beneath a thin layer of ash. Somehow the magic in the flute had been released as it burned, turning the sticks into pure gold.

The vagabond will never have to beg again. The fortune he now possesses is sufficient enough to make kings envious.

The vagabond is now aware that his piping on the wizard's flute had caused the torments that visited the land. He uses his wealth to restore homes and land damaged by the pestilences. Because of his magnanimous nature, he is now famous as well as wealthy. The vagabond lives in happiness, but he never forgets the miseries of a beggar's life, nor the day when wizard, creature, and flute changed his life forever. ≡

Glossary

Words often have more than one definition. We've listed only the meaning used in the story. You can learn more ways to use the word by checking a dictionary.

Aback—to surprise somebody and make him unsure how to react
Abates—lessens; diminishes
Abject—without hope of improvement
Abode—a house or home; a dwelling
Abolishes—outlaws something; puts an end to
Absconded—run away especially secretively
Abyss—a chasm or gorge that is extremely deep or vast; endless space; terrible situation
Addled— confused; unable to think logically
Afflicted—sick; suffering from pain or distress
Agitate—make someone anxious; move something violently
Ailing — sickly
Aims— plans; intends to
Alas—an expression of sorrow, grief, or concern
Alms—charitable donations usually money but could be food or clothing
Anoints—bless someone with oil or water, usually part of a religious ceremony like baptism, in this case *anoints* is used in an ironic way meaning that *anoints* is used in opposition to its actual definition; here it is used to mean *carelessly spilled*; humor often uses irony
Apple-pie order— a phrase meaning to have everything just so; in an exact way or following a precise method
Apprenticeship—the time spent by someone (called an apprentice) to learn a trade from an expert in the chosen occupation
Arcane—mysteriously obscure, requiring secret knowledge to understand
Archaeologist—someone who studies ancient cultures through remains, usually by digging to find bones, pottery, and building foundations.
Ascent—climb; rising up a hill
Ascertain— determine; figure out
Assails—overwhelms the mind or senses
Assemblage—a collection of people or things
Astonished—speechless with surprise; stunned
Astounded—greatly amazed; tremendously surprised

Asunder—into different parts or pieces

Awe — fear mixed with admiration

Awry—crooked; amiss; events didn't go as planned

Baffle—puzzle; hinder; bewilder

Banished—forced to leave one's country; exiled; driven away

Barren—bare of vegetation

Befall—come to pass; occur; happen

Bejeweled—adorned with jewels or gems

Bellows—1. yells; 2. a piece of equipment for producing air under pressure, an example is the device used for making a fire burn hotter

Bemoan—to express grief or disappointment about something

Benefactor—supporter; contributor especially one who gives money

Beset—troubled by

Bewitched—charmed so much as to take away the power of resistance

Bide—bear or endure something

Bids—commands

Billowing—rising and rolling in large waves

Bleary—dimmed with tears; misty; indistinct

Boils—inflamed, painful swellings of the skin caused by infection

Bolt of cloth—a long length of material for making clothing which comes wrapped around itself or a heavy cardboard support

Bolt upright—suddenly straighten up

Boneyard— a slang word for graveyard; cemetery

Bore—past tense of *bear*; sustained the burden of; underwent something heavy or difficult

Brackish—somewhat salty; a mixture of fresh and salt water; sometimes water which is still (a puddle or pond) becomes brackish by leaching salt from the soil.

Breached—break down an obstruction to allow something through

Brigand—an armed robber operating in wild or isolated terrain, usually as a member of a roving band but not always

Brimstone—sulfur which smells like rotten eggs

Brink—the very edge of something; could be the edge of a place or the edge of understanding

Brisk—active; lively

Bulk—large mass; body of great size

Butt—object of ridicule or contempt; as in "He was the *butt* of their joke."

Callused—thickened skin; usually on the palms of the hands or the bottom of the feet, calluses occur where there is friction over a period of time

Canopied—a covering put above the bed; canopies can be purely for decoration or can serve functions as well like keeping heat in and light and insects out.

Carnegie Hall—America's premier concert hall. Named after its original benefactor, Andrew Carnegie, the hall was built in 1891 in New York City. Only world-class musicians perform there.

Cauldron—a large metal pot for boiling liquids; a large kettle; can also be spelled *caldron*

Chafed— became sore or worn from rubbing

Character—reputation; essential quality; nature; moral make-up

Charade—an absurdly false or pointless act or situation

Churning out—completing many things quickly

Clouds—obscures

Coffers—a supply or store of money; strongboxes or chests used for keeping valuables or money safe

Comely—pleasant to look at; attractive

Comply—to obey or conform to something like a rule, law, wish, or regulation

Comprehend—understand

Confection—something sweet to eat; for example: cookies, candy, rolls, buns, or donuts

Confinement—a restriction or limitation of boundaries or scope

Conjuring—performing magic tricks

Conservative clothing—modest clothing in older styles, usually in solid, sober colors like blue, gray, and black

Converge—gather at a point

Corset—a stiffened garment to shape the waist and bust

Crenellations—square indentations in a building to provide protective places for firing weapons; originally used to protect archers

Crevice—a deep split or opening, especially in rock

Cudgel—a short, heavy stick used as a weapon

Culinary—having to do with the kitchen or cooking

Curries—grooms or rubs down an animal, usually a horse

Cutthroats—murders; killers; violent bullies

Defoliate—to strip a plant of its leaves
Dehydration—the state of being dry or without water
Delectable—delightful; delicious
Depiction—a picture, sculpture or description of something
Destitute—without the necessities of life like food and shelter
Detrimental—harmful
Disheveled—rumpled; tousled; in disarray
Dismay—a feeling of disappointment or hopelessness
Distribute—scatter evenly over a surface
Doggedly—stubbornly; persistently
Douses—pours water over; drenches with liquid
Downs—pours; swallows quickly
Dunes—hills formed by wind-blown sand

Eked—made with difficulty
Eluding—escaping
Elixir—a miraculous drink that cures all ailments; a sweetened preparation of medicine; a substance which prolongs life indefinitely
Emanating—emitting; sending out
Embossed—a raised pattern on a surface
Enchantment—magic spell
Encroaching—trespassing or invading a boundary whether authority, rights, or property
Enraged—made furiously angry; inflame
Enshrouded—veiled; wrapped in; obscured
Ensuing—following as a result of (a previous action)
Enthralled—captivated; put under a spell
Estate—an individually owned piece of property containing a residence usually large and expensive to maintain
Etching—recording something to a permanent surface, usually by scratching or using acid to mark the surface; in this case used to describe how carefully Joseph is remembering each detail
Ethic—a moral or principle of human behavior
Evicted—forced out
Exact—force to pay; demand
Excavation—uncover by digging; unearth
Exceedingly—without limit or measure
Exertions—hard efforts; activity involving great physical labor
Exile—banish from a country or home

Expel—force to leave; drive out
Extracts—pulls out with effort

Fare—food
Fate—principle believed to predetermine events; destiny
Fathom—understand something
Famished—starving; extremely hungry
Feigning—faking
Ferreted—sought out with great persistence and care
Fetid—rotten smelling; stinking
Feverishly—in an excited or agitated manner
Fickleness—changeable; unstable; variable
Fiendish, Fiendishly—malicious(ly); with cunning and wickedness
Figment—made up or imaginary
Flabbergasted—totally surprised or amazed someone
Flagon—a container for beverages characterized by a handle, a narrow neck with a spout and, sometimes, a lid.
Flung—past tense of fling; spread out quickly; thrown fast
Foliage—leaves of a plant
Folly—foolish; thoughtless; with a lack of understanding or sense
Fond—having affection toward; likes
Formulating—to express or define something in a detailed and systematic way; to plan carefully
Franticly— (can also be spelled *frantically*) in an excited, confused manner, usually accompanied by a highly emotional state due to anger, fear, worry, or pain
Frenzied—wildly excited; characterized by uncontrolled emotion
Fret—worry
Frittered—to waste something like time or money
Frolic; Frolicking—play happily; be merry and full of laughter
Fruitless—didn't achieve anything; no use; unsuccessful

Gapes—opens; splits apart forming a gap
Gaunt—extremely thin; emaciated; looking very bony
Glacial—frigid; icy; cold and hostile
Gnaw—bite or chew persistently
Gravelly—a grating, rough-sounding thing
Gribit—the sound a frog makes
Gruel—a thin porridge made of cooked grain in water or milk

Guffaw—to laugh loudly; an unpleasant, loud, and coarse laughter
Gusto—keen enthusiasm; zest; with much energy

Haggles—arguing over price or terms
Hastens—to go somewhere quickly
Heady—intoxicating
Herbivore—a creature that eats plants only
Hew—to cut or chop with an edged tool like an ax
Hideous—very ugly; revolting to look at
His heart was in his throat — a phrase meaning he was very excited and fearful at the same time
Hobbles—walks slowly and unsteadily, taking short steps
Homestead—a farm; a house with outbuildings and land
Hooligans—young criminals or ruffians
Horizon—the line in which the earth and sky seem to meet
Hostility—strong opposition; ill will; unfriendliness
Hue—a specific shade of color; tint
Hydrated—combined with water; people require a certain amount of water in their bodies to remain healthy
Hypnotic—causing a sleep or trance-like state

Ichor—an acrid, thin watery discharge as from a wound
Idle—unoccupied; unemployed; lazy
Illusion—a false idea or belief; an unreal or deceptive appearance
Imbued—filled the mind with a quality or belief; saturated; permeated
Impervious—cannot be penetrated or passed through
Industrious—hard-working; diligent
Infectious—catching; affecting the emotions of others
Inferno—a fierce fire or place that is burning with great flames and heat
Infuriates—angers; makes someone furious
Innovative—having the quality of taking a new approach to something; changing something to make it new
Invincible—cannot be beat or overcome

Jaunt—a short trip for pleasure
Jostles—bumps about; shakes

Keel over—fall over from exhaustion or illness; collapse
Knave—a dishonest, cunning man; a male servant

Lady-in-waiting—female attendant for a queen or princess
Lair—an animal's den; a protected resting place
Laments—expresses grief or sorrow about something; mourns; regrets
Languishing—losing strength; fading; becoming less vital or successful
Lapse—pass by; a passage of time
Larcenous—being a thief; having the intention of or actually stealing
Lax—loose; relaxed; not strict
Leafs—turns the pages of a book quickly
Lest—a conjunction connecting a precaution to a result; for example
"watch where you step *lest* you stumble"
Lichen—a group of algae and fungus living together on a rock or tree
Liege—lord; under feudal law a ruler who provided protection and justice in return for the right to loyal service by his subjects
Lintel—the horizontal supporting beam over a window or door
List—to lean to one side
Livid—very angry; furious
Looms—takes shape; sees a large, indistinct shape as through fog or mist, sometimes a threatening or menacing shape
Lulls—quiet times; breaks in activity; a calm period of time
Lure—to entice or tempt; to attract or persuade

Magnanimous—noble minded; generous in forgiving insult or injury
Magnitude—greatness of size
Maiden—young unmarried woman
Malevolence—wishing ill or harm to others; having evil intent
Malicious; Maliciously—spiteful(ly); deliberately causing harm or pain to others
Mammoth—extremely large; enormous
Mane—a large amount of thick long hair on somebody's head
Marvels—is amazed, impressed or surprised by something
Maw—the mouth of a predatory animal
Meadow—a grassy field
Meager—unsatisfactory in quantity; very small
Medallions—large medals; decorated metal disks
Mere—exactly what is specified; nothing more than
Mete—to distribute in a measured way; allot
Mewling—crying; whimpering
Miasma—harmful vapor arising from dead or decaying plant or animal

tissue
Midst—center; middle
Minutest—the very smallest; extremely fine; exact
Mirth—laughter; merriment
Mock—pretend; done as an act particularly for amusement
Molested—meddled with so as to cause harm; annoyed; pestered
Molten—melted into liquid, usually used in reference to rock as in "The *molten* lava runs down the slope of the volcano."
Mountebank—a traveling seller of questionable medicine; a fake healer
Mournfully—sadly
Muck—filth; trash; manure
Murmurs—complains secretly; says something quietly
Muses—puzzles over; ponders about; meditates on
Mustering—to gather; collect; assemble together

Nary – not one; none
Nauseating—causing one to feel sick; causing the urge to vomit
Nay—no; refusal
Newt—a small amphibian of the salamander family
Nod—a quick lowering and raising of the head used to show agreement or recognition
Noisome—offensive to the senses; foul smelling

Oaths—curses
Odious—disgusting; hateful; offensive
Odiferous – giving off a strong scent
Ousted—removed somebody from an office or position
Overwhelmed—overpowered somebody emotionally; crushed

Partake—to eat or drink particularly in the company of others
Patron saint—a saint believed to be a special guardian of something or somebody, for example: Saint Francis of Assisi for animals, St. Christopher for travelers; St. Vincent de Paul for charity
Peculiar—unusual; strange
Pell-mell—a disorderly mess; rushing around in confusion
Persevere—stubbornly continuing an action in the face of adversity
Pestilence—a highly contagious fatal disease or anything considered harmful or evil
Pharaoh—the title of the rulers of ancient Egypt

Phenomenon—something or someone who is extraordinary; out of the ordinary

Pilfer—steal in small quantity, usually items of little value

Pities—feels sorry for; feels mercy or forgiveness toward someone who has done wrong

Plods—walk slowly and heavily

Ploy—an action or tactic meant to outwit or deceive another person

Plummets—falls rapidly; drops straight down

Pox—any of a number of diseases that cause blistering of the skin; wishing a *pox* on someone is to hope that misfortune visits that person

Prank—a practical joke; mischievous trick

Predicament—a situation for which there is no clear solution, often dangerous, difficult, embarrassing, unpleasant, or, occasionally, comical

Pretext—false excuse; made-up reason

Profusely— pouring forth freely; abundantly; generously

Proffering; proffers—offers something to be accepted by another; holds something out for another to take

Prominent—jutting; conspicuous; noticeable right away

Prospect—something that is expected to happen in the future

Prospecting — searching for gold or other precious metals, oil, or gems

Prostrate—to lay with face toward the ground; to make or grow weak as in "he was *prostrated* by illness"

Pummel – hit repeatedly; beat someone or something usually using fists

Putrid—rotten and giving off a revolting smell

Pyre—a heap of burning materials as in "a funeral *pyre*"

Quavering—trembling sound caused by nervousness or fear

Quiche—a hearty pie made with an egg and milk filling with additions of various meats and vegetables

Rally—to gather or collect either people, things, or qualities like strength or health

Rants—speaks in a loud way usually repetitively and for a long time

Realm—kingdom

Recollection—memory; remembering something

Recuperating—regaining health and strength

Regale—to entertain with amusing stories

Reins—straps used to control the movements of a horse

Relinquishes—surrenders something; resigns; abandons; lets go

Remnants—a small part left over; a trace of what once was there

Renowned—famous

Rent—a rip or tear in a surface

Repast—meal; food

Reproof—tell somebody off; rebuke; chide

Resonance—increasing and strengthening of sound by sympathetic vibration

Saga—a long story or journey

Sated—filled up completely; fully satisfied, usually used with regard to food or other desires

Salivating—producing excessive amounts of saliva

Salve—a soothing lotion; anything that heals as in "Her words were a *salve* to my heart."

Sarcophagus—a stone coffin usually decorated with writing and fancy designs

Savor—enjoy the taste of something

Scorcher—burning hot

Scrumptious—delicious; first rate

Sentry—guard; a military person who watches for danger usually at an entrance to or exit from a protected area

Shackles—metal bracelets for holding prisoners, usually connected by a chain

Shadowing—constantly following someone

Sheepishly—timidly; in an embarrassed manner

Sheers—shaves or clips with scissors

Shoo—chase away; an interjection to drive an animal or person away

Shrewdly—cleverly; astutely

Shuns—consistently avoids something or somebody

Skirmish—a brief fight

Skits—short comical plays

Slink—sneak; to move quietly and secretively

Slosh—spill or splash liquid clumsily

Smelted—melted ore to make metal

Smoldering – burning slowing without flame

Sling—a weapon used for throwing a stone consisting of a strap in which the stone is twirled before being launched

Sodden—soaked; totally wet

Sovereign—an old British gold coin worth one pound

Spawns—produces or is the source of something
Squatters—people who illegally occupy land
Staunchly— (can also be spelled *stanchly*) steadily; loyally; solidly
Stench—a really offensive odor, usually a strong lingering one
Stouthearted—courageous; unyielding; brave
Stride — to *"take something in stride"* is to cope with a difficult or un-usual situation easily
Studious—fond of study; diligent; earnest; eager
Succulent—really juicy
Suitor — a man who tries to persuade a woman to marry him
Sulfurous—like burning sulfur in terms of color and smell
Sulkily—in a bad mood and refusing to talk because of resentment; cross
Sullied—made dirty; stained; tarnished; spoiled
Superstitious—believing in charms and omens; based on a belief which is not proven by the laws of science
Surmises—guesses; drawing a conclusion based on limited evidence
Sward—a grassy area like in a park
Swayed—switch direction or sides; persuaded to do something different
Swigs—drink in large gulps
Swills—drinks greedily especially alcoholic beverages
Swindler—a person who cheats another person by deceiving them
Swoons—faints

Tale—a short fictional story
Tankard—a large drinking mug usually for beer
Tepid—somewhat warm
Therapeutic—used to treat disease and restore health
Thy—your
Toil; Toiling—working very hard
Tomes—very thick, heavy books
Torrid—very hot
Trample—damage something by stepping on it
Trek—make a long hard journey
Triumphantly—victoriously; successfully
Trudges— walk with slow heavy steps
Trundles—a slow, heavy rolling movement
Turmoil—confusion; disturbance
Tutelage—teaching
Tyrant—a cruel dominating ruler with absolute power

Uncanny—unusual; unexpected; mysterious
Unscathed—not damaged in any way
Uproariously—loud; rowdy; noisy

Vagabond—a tramp; a homeless beggar
Vented—released
Verge—edge; boundary; margin
Veritable—genuine; true; actual
Vermin—pests; people who are wicked, destructive, and undesirable
Vessel—a container for liquids
Victoriously—in a victorious manner; celebrating having won a contest
Victuals—food; provisions
Vile—wicked; evil
Vivacious—lively; active; high-spirited
Vogue—the fashion at a particular time

Waft—float gently through the air
Waif—a thin, fragile-looking child; an abandoned child
Waylays—lies in wait for somebody in order to ambush or rob them
Wellspring—a plentiful source of something
Whilst—a British alternative for "while"
Wickedly expensive—so very costly as to be absurd
Wits—intelligence; reasoning power; cleverness
Wizened—dried up; shriveled; wrinkled
Wallow—immerse yourself in something; fully enjoy something
Wondrous—amazing; exciting wonder
Writhes—twists or contorts the body as in extreme pain
Wrought—past tense of *work;* made

Meet the author

Mack finds inspiration for his stories everywhere and carries a notebook and pen to record them. He is a graduate of the University of Maryland and a world traveler who enjoys learning new things. His other passions include weightlifting, music, and the large organic garden he tends with his wife, Celia.

Meet the illustrator

Celia loves creating beauty of all kinds. She is an award-winning photographer and a multimedia artist. Celia earned a degree in Business from Indiana University, Bloomington, Indiana and in Systems Engineering from the Naval Postgraduate School, Monterey, California. A renaissance woman, she is also a co-inventor of a patented antenna design. Celia served 21 years as an officer in the U.S. Army. She now enjoys gardening and creating books with her husband, Mack.

Thank you for reading this Pilinut Press book. We hope you enjoyed it! For the release schedule of more new books, please visit our website at www.pilinutpress.com. Releases coming soon include:

Illustrated Tales:

Little Bianca

Little Bianca, a bright-eyed two-year-old, lives with her Poppa who is an artist. Bianca's overworked Poppa tries to eke out a living by selling the art he produces in his art gallery. Poppa has masterpieces for sale, but no one seems to be interested.

Times are hard for Bianca and her Poppa. They may soon find themselves hungry and living on the streets. Little Bianca wants to help her distressed Poppa. Can she think of an idea that will help her Poppa put food on the table and save his art gallery?

Webb's Wondrous Tales Book 2

More stories of the fantastic and fascinating.

Can You Keep a Secret?

Ricky has the biggest ears in town and overhears everyone's conversations. He also likes to repeat what he hears. What can the townsfolk do to keep Ricky from spreading their secrets?

Health and Fitness:

Small Gym, Big Workout

Packed with detailed information, Small Gym, Big Workout guides you through the layout and set up of your home gym. Imagine monster workouts, muscle toning, and weight loss, all in an area of less than 165 square feet! No, that is not a typo. Lack of space is no longer an issue in setting up your home gym.

Printed in the United States
76773LV00002B/103-144

9 780977 957613